PRAISE FOR CHRIS RYAN:

'Gripping from the off'
Sun

'SAS hero Chris Ryan sets a cracking pace'
Lovereading

'Fast-paced action thriller
that hits all the right spots'
The Bookseller

'Chris Ryan proves, once again,
that he is a master of suspense'
Waterstones Books Quarterly

CHRIS RYAN
SAS HERO

- Joined the SAS in 1984, serving in military hot zones across the world.

- Expert in overt and covert operations in war zones, including Northern Ireland, Africa, the Middle East and other classified territories.

- Commander of the Sniper squad within the anti-terrorist team.

- Part of an 8 man patrol on the Bravo Two Zero Gulf War mission in Iraq.

- The mission was compromised. 3 fellow soldiers died, and 4 more were captured as POWs. Ryan was the only person to defy the enemy, evading capture and escaping to Syria on foot over a distance of 300 kilometres.

- His ordeal made history as the longest escape and evasion by an SAS trooper, for which he was awarded the Military Medal.

- His books are dedicated to the men and women who risk their lives fighting for the armed forces.

- You can find Chris on Twitter @exSASChrisRyan

CHRIS RYAN

AGENT 21
CODEBREAKER

RED FOX

*Available by Chris Ryan and published
by Random House Children's Publishers UK:*

The One That Got Away

AGENT 21 series
Agent 21
Agent 21: Reloaded
Agent 21: Codebreaker

CODE RED series
Flash Flood
Wildfire
Outbreak
Vortex
Twister
Battleground

ALPHA FORCE series
Survival
Rat-Catcher
Desert Pursuit
Hostage
Red Centre
Hunted
Blood Money
Fault Line
Black Gold
Untouchable

Published by the Random House Group for adult readers:

NON-FICTION
The One That Got Away
Chris Ryan's SAS Fitness Book
Chris Ryan's Ultimate Survival Guide
Fight to Win: Deadly Skills of the Elite Forces

FICTION
Stand By, Stand By
Zero Option
The Kremlin Device
Tenth Man Down
Hit List
The Watchman
Land of Fire
Greed
The Increment
Blackout
Ultimate Weapon
Strike Back
Firefight
Who Dares Wins
One Good Turn (Adult Quick Read for World Book Day 2008)

AGENT 21
CODEBREAKER

AGENT 21: CODEBREAKER

AGENT 21: CODEBREAKER
A RED FOX BOOK 978 1 849 41009 0

First published in Great Britain by Red Fox,
an imprint of Random House Children's Publishers UK
A Random House Group Company
This edition published 2013

9 10 8

Set in Adobe Garamond

Red Fox Books are published by Random House Children's Publishers UK,
61–63 Uxbridge Road, London W5 5SA

www.**randomhousechildrens**.co.uk
www.**totallyrandombooks**.co.uk
www.**randomhouse**.co.uk

Addresses for companies within The Random House Group Limited
can be found at: www.randomhouse.co.uk/offices.htm

THE RANDOM HOUSE GROUP Limited Reg. No. 954009

A CIP catalogue record for this book is available from the British Library.

Penguin Random House is committed to a sustainable future for
our business, our readers and our planet. This book is made from
Forest Stewardship Council® certified paper.

Printed and bound in Great Britain by Clays Ltd, Elcograf S.p.A.

CONTENTS

Prologue: Northern Ireland, 1973   1

1. The Wrong Place at the Wrong Time   11
2. Advance/Retreat   19
3. Green Light   39
4. Room 7   51
5. Hidden in Plain Sight   67
6. The Puzzle Master   82
7. The Second Bomb   94
8. St Oswald's   100
9. Casualty of War   117
10. 00:00:00   128
11. Dishonourable Discharge   141
12. NY Hero   159
13. Liquid Lunch   176
14. Tilt Switch   192
15. Hangman   203
16. Evorgdul   221
17. The Graveyard Shift   237
18. The Long-tailed Shrike   257
19. Chalker Mews   269
20. Blackout   283
21. Murder in his Eyes   303

Epilogue: One Week Later   315

AGENT 21

Real name: Zak Darke

Known pseudonyms: Harry Gold, Jason Cole

Age: 15

Date of birth: March 27

Parents: Al and Janet Darke [DECEASED]

Operational skills: Weapons handling, navigation, excellent facility with languages, excellent computer and technical skills.

Previous operations: (1) Inserted under cover into the compound of Mexican drug magnate Cesar Martinez Toledo. Befriended target's son Cruz. Successfully supplied evidence of target's illegal activities. Successfully guided commando team in to compound. Target eliminated. (2) Inserted into Angola to place explosive device on suspected terrorist ship, the the *MV Mercantile*. Vessel destroyed, Agent 21 extracted.

AGENT 17

Real name: classified

Known pseudonyms: 'Gabriella', 'Gabs'

Age: 27

Operational skills: Advanced combat and self-defence, surveillance, tracking.

Currently charged with ongoing training of Agent 21 on remote Scottish island of St Peter's Crag.

AGENT 16

Real name: classified

Known pseudonyms: 'Raphael', 'Raf'

Age: 30

Operational skills: Advanced combat and self-defence, sub-aqua, land-vehicle control.

Currently charged with ongoing training of Agent 21 on remote Scottish island of St Peter's Crag.

'MICHAEL'

Real name: classified

Known pseudonyms: 'Mr Bartholomew'

Age: classified

Recruited Agent 21 after death of his parents.
Currently his handler. Has links with MI5, but
represents a classified government agency.

CRUZ MARTINEZ (presumed dead)

Age: 17

Significant information: Succeeded Cesar Martinez
as head of largest Mexican drug cartel.
Thought to blame Agent 21 for death of
father. Highly intelligent. Profile remained
low since coming to power. Thought to have
drowned during sinking of *MV Mercantile*.

PROLOGUE

Northern Ireland. 18 June, 1973

'County Armagh? Oh, it's as pretty as a picture.'

That's what old Mrs Herder told her sons, and she was right. It *is* as pretty as a picture. Unless you're a member of the British Army, in which case it's hell on earth.

Lee Herder doesn't notice the scenery. He's blind to the little cobbled streets and the tiny cottages in this sleepy village of Ballycork. Blind to the cotton-wool clouds in an otherwise blue sky. All he sees is the group of Parachute Regiment soldiers, twelve of them, each carrying an L64 assault rifle as they keep a fifty-metre cordon around the central square. In the middle of the square is a stone monument to the fallen of two world wars, and a white Ford Capri.

Lee looks to his right. His older brother Richard – Sonny to their late mum and dad, Dick to

1

everybody else – is there. The two brothers are dressed the same. Blast-resistant body armour on the outside of their standard-issue camouflage gear. Helmet. A belt containing the tools the two brothers need to disarm the car bomb under the Capri.

From the edge of the cordon, Lee sees a bird land on the driver's-side wing mirror of the vehicle. Black and white wings. Green rump. He recognizes it as a chaffinch.

'Let's hope Tweetie Pie doesn't hop onto the pressure plate,' Dick says. 'Could be noisy.'

Lee nods as they pass through the Paras' cordon. This is their third car bomb in as many days. They were good bomb-disposal guys before their tour to Northern Ireland. Now they're just about the best. But being the best doesn't calm your nerves before each new job. No two devices are the same, and bomb-makers take pride in inventing clever booby traps for guys like Lee and Dick.

Clever ways to kill them.

They are kneeling down by the car now, staring at the rear wheel. Sweat trickles down the back of Lee's neck. Whoever called this one in did well to notice the tiny triggers, one just in front of the tyre, one just behind it. Each trigger is made from a tiny ball of Blu-tack, sandwiched between two iron nails. Each nail has a wire attached to it. As soon as the car moves forward or backwards, the tyre will squash one of the triggers. The nails will touch and complete the circuit. Bang.

Defusing it is not going to be straightforward. The wires leading from each nail are taut, which rings alarm bells in the brothers' minds.

'Motion sensor?' Lee suggests.

'Motion sensor,' his brother agrees.

They lie on their bellies as Dick shines a torch under the car. Sure enough, fifty centimetres in, a metal ring – no bigger than a wedding band – surrounds each bare wire. Lee remembers a game their dad had built for them when they were kids – a wiggly wire connected to a battery and a buzzer. You had to move a metal loop from one end of the wire to the other. If they touched, the buzzer would sound and you had to go back to the beginning. Same idea here, only there's no buzzer and no starting again. The rings are connected to a mess of wires fixed to the undercarriage of the car, and the mess of wires is connected to enough bright orange Semtex plastic explosive to send the car sky high. He smiles as he wonders what his dad would say now if he could see them using their skills today. And he wishes – not for the first time – that their mum and dad had not been so cruelly taken from them, courtesy of a drunken teenage driver one wet night.

The brothers look at each other now. 'Controlled explosion?' Lee says. Dick nods. This device is crude and simple, but they can be the most difficult. The slightest movement will detonate the explosives. They stand up and walk back to the cordon.

An officer is waiting for them with an expectant look on his face. A glance at his stripes tell the brothers he's in charge. 'Well?' he asks.

'You need to evacuate everyone within a two-hundred-metre radius,' Dick tells him. 'It's too risky to defuse and there's a lot of orange cake under there. We'll need to carry out a controlled explosion.'

Dick is already turning away when the officer says: 'No.'

The two brothers give him a dangerous look.

'What do you mean?' Dick says.

'I have my orders. The IRA will get almost as much attention if that thing explodes *without* killing anybody.'

'Don't be so bloody stupid,' Lee says. 'It's booby-trapped . . . too dangerous . . .'

'Fine.' The officer is looking around now, as if hunting for someone else. 'If you two aren't up to the job, we'll bring in somebody who is.'

Lee glances at his brother. He knows they're both thinking the same thing: there's nobody else in the

British Army even half as qualified as them. It's not arrogance. It's just the truth. Do as the rupert says and send in another bomb-disposal guy and it would be sending them to their death.

Dick swears under his breath. 'Get these soldiers further back,' he says, talking not to the Para but to Lee.

'Mate . . .' Lee starts to say, but he doesn't finish. His brother is already walking back to the car, his gait stiff on account of his protective gear. Lee thinks about calling after him, but doesn't. He knows his brother too well. When his mind is made up, it's made up. Instead he shouts to the Paras, 'OK, everyone, move back! *Move back!* It's a big one . . .'

The soldiers don't move. It takes a barked instruction from the officer to make them retreat. By now, Dick has reached the Ford Capri. He's lying on his back and is slowly easing himself under the car, like a mechanic. Lee can see nothing but his protective boots sticking out from underneath. He realizes he's holding his breath.

A cloud passes in front of the sun. Lee feels a chill. He tells himself to stay calm. Dick taught him everything he knows about bomb disposal, and what his brother *doesn't* know isn't worth knowing.

A minute passes.

Two.

Movement. Lee startles. The chaffinch has returned, only now it's not perched on the side mirror. It's pecking at something on the road, fifty metres from his own position, but only a hand's breadth away from one of the triggers. Lee wants to shout out, but he stops himself. The last thing his brother needs is a sudden surprise. Instead he takes a step forward, hoping to frighten away the little bird.

He can hear his own pulse as he takes another step.

And another.

The bird stops pecking and looks up. It stares at Lee, its head slightly cocked, as though listening carefully.

'Fly away, birdie,' Lee breathes.

But the bird doesn't fly away. It stays where it is, inches from the trigger, still staring.

And so Lee takes another step forward.

It's the worst mistake he's ever made. The chaffinch does move, but in the wrong direction. It scuttles towards the undercarriage of the car.

Three things happen almost at once.

Lee shouts. He can't help himself. '*NO!*'

The chaffinch knocks the wire leading from the detonator.

And the car explodes.

The noise of the explosion is ear-splitting. The thought crosses Lee's mind, as he is thrown backwards five metres by the thunderous, pulsating shock waves, that it must surely be audible from thirty miles away. As he lands with a thump onto the cobbles, he feels a strange regret for the death of the chaffinch. But it is only as the dust starts to fall that the brutal truth hits him, harder than any shrapnel.

His brother.

Lee pushes himself up to his feet and staggers through the dust cloud, unable to see clearly more than a couple of metres, but aware of a fiery glow where the Ford Capri had been. The closer he comes, the brighter it glows. And hotter too. When he is five metres away, he stops and falls to his knees. The heat scorches the skin of his face even underneath his mask, but Lee doesn't care about that. He finds himself praying that his brother had managed miraculously to escape before the detonation, but he knows that's a vain hope. And it's not only because he witnessed the moment of the blast.

It's because two metres from where he kneels he can see the stump of a dismembered leg, burning like a well-seasoned log on a winter's night.

It's all that remains of Dick 'Sonny' Herder, the finest bomb-disposal guy Her Majesty's army had to offer . . .

THE PRESENT DAY

15 JUNE

1

THE WRONG PLACE AT THE WRONG TIME

'Are you here to kill me?'

The boy's voice didn't sound scared. Curious, if anything. And calm. Ready for what was to come.

Agent 21 peered through the darkness. In his right hand he held a 9mm snubnose and he knew, if it came to it, that his hand would be steady.

'Because if you're going to kill me,' the boy continued, 'please do it quickly. A shot to the head should do it. I won't feel that.'

A pause.

'At least, I don't *think* I will,' he said.

Agent 21 gripped the handgun a little harder. The safety was off. The weapon was loaded.

He'd had no idea when he'd woken up that morning that this was how his day would turn out.

* * *

But then, *nobody* had any idea when they woke up that morning how the day would turn out. Not least Amelia Howard who, eighteen hours earlier, had left her home in Brixton in order to catch the first train into central London.

Amelia had been making this journey every day for the past nine years. She often noticed that the other commuters who joined her on the platform looked a good deal less happy than she was to be up at this early hour. It was always the same faces, and the faces were always the same: gloomy, tired, un-enthusiastic. Amelia was the opposite. She enjoyed her job working at a children's home in Islington. Oh, it didn't pay very well, but she felt as though she was making a difference, and that was what mattered.

The arrival of the train was preceded by a rush of air from the tunnel. It messed Amelia's hair, but that didn't worry her. She was pretty, but not the type to worry too much about her appearance. While other women on the tube held tiny make-up mirrors to their faces and fixed their lipstick, Amelia was more likely to be lost in a book. It made the journey pass more quickly.

The train thundered into the station and the doors hissed open. Amelia stepped into one of the middle carriages and took a seat. A man in a suit sat on her right, an older woman on her left. Amelia took her book from her handbag, placed the bag behind her feet and started to read.

It was her habit to look up from the pages every time the train slowed down. That way, she could see each stop slide into view and keep track of where she was on her journey. So it was that she saw Brixton become Stockwell, where she immersed herself once more in her book, then Stockwell became Vauxhall, and she looked up a minute later as the train slowed down on its approach to Pimlico.

But Amelia did not realize she had already seen Pimlico station for the last time.

The explosion that rocked the train was immense. It shocked Amelia in two distinct ways. First, the noise. There was a series of eruptions in quick succession, each one sounding like a firework detonating an inch from her ear. And then the movement. She felt the train derailing, then a moment of sudden nausea as the front of the carriage rose two metres in the air.

The lights went out. Amelia could only see on account of the sparks outside as the carriage scraped against the tunnel wall. By that faint orange light, she could see the terror in the faces of her fellow passengers as they gripped the arms of their seats tightly.

The screaming started at about the same time that the walls of the carriage buckled. What had seemed so tough and sturdy crumpled like tinfoil and burned like paper. The glass windows cracked and shattered. Amelia had never seen anybody die before, but now, by the scant light of the sparks, she saw a shard of twisted metal drill into the chest of the woman sitting next to her, and felt the splatter of blood on her face. Amelia fell forward onto the floor.

The train had been moving all this time, but now it came to a halt. There was a moment of sinister silence – the passengers had stopped screaming – and it was utterly dark. Amelia groped around for her handbag with trembling hands. When she found it, she pulled out her mobile phone and turned it on. The screen glowed, lighting up the gruesome sight of the dead woman who had also fallen to the floor, and whose dead eyes were staring up at her.

Amelia wasn't the only person to light up a phone. All along the carriage, screens glowed like little beacons. They dimly revealed a scene of total devastation – and Amelia's neighbour wasn't the only dead body: she saw the grey silhouettes of corpses all around. She looked at the back of her hand. A shard of glass from one of the shattered windows had sliced it open and blood was slipping down onto the sleeve of her lightweight jacket.

Little by little, the soft sound of weeping filled the carriage. Amelia staggered to her feet – not easy, because the floor of the train was at an incline. 'We . . . we should move to the front of the carriage,' she called out shakily.

Nobody heard her. Because as she spoke there was an immense groaning sound from up above. Cold dread surged through Amelia's veins. The sound was like nothing she had ever heard before and something told her that the end was near.

Her whole body was shaking as she lifted her phone above her head and looked up. The roof of the carriage was sagging and buckled. It was on the point of collapsing.

'Oh my God,' she whispered. She looked along the carriage. The sagging roof extended as far as she could see.

The groaning sound again. Louder this time. The roof sagged a little more.

Amelia Howard was not a religious woman. She hadn't been to church since she was a child. But now she fell to her knees with her head bowed, and whispered a prayer. She knew she was going to die and so she didn't pray for life. She simply prayed that her death wouldn't hurt too much.

She was still praying when the roof collapsed,

but her prayer was not answered. Countless tons of rubble crushed down on top of her. She felt the unspeakable agony of bones breaking along her spine while her arms and legs shattered like brittle twigs. Her head was crushed between the floor of the carriage and the weight above her. She screamed in pain, but the scream was muffled by her coffin of earth. She tried to breathe in, but instead of air she swallowed a throatful of dust. Her mouth filled up with blood and the world went dim.

The end, when it came, was a mercy. Not just for Amelia Howard, but for everybody else in her carriage, who just happened to be in the wrong place, at the wrong time.

The emergency services were speedy and efficient. But there was very little they could do.

Within minutes of the blast, the entire tube network had been evacuated. A cordon had been fixed around Pimlico Station. Ambulances, police cars and fire appliances clogged the surrounding roads, and the sirens of others approaching filled the air. Rescue workers wearing hard hats and oxygen masks bravely strode down the underpass that led into the station. Others walked out, their clothes and skin covered in grime and their faces utterly shocked. None of them had ever seen such sights before.

There were other vehicles too. Unmarked SUVs from which plainclothes anti-terrorist officers exited with grim faces. Helicopters circled up above. A news crew had already arrived and was forcing its way through the crowd of onlookers standing by the cordon while five police officers shouted at them to keep their distance. One man, however – he had shoulder-length grey hair, green eyes and smelled of cherry tobacco – approached the cordon, lifted it over his head and stepped towards the blast site. A police officer ran up to him and was clearly just about to scream at him to get back behind the cordon when the man waved an ID card in his face.

The police officer's eyes widened and he stood almost to attention. 'All right, sir. Please go on.'

The grey-haired man gave the policeman a vague nod, then continued towards the underpass. When he was five metres away, he stopped. He looked lost in thought as he watched the fledgling rescue operation unfold. When it became clear that the emergency services were not carrying out the living on their stretchers, but the dead, he bowed his head, sighed and walked back to the cordon.

'Can I be of assistance, Mr Bartholomew?' asked the officer who had tried to stop him coming in.

Mr Bartholomew smiled a wan, thankful smile.

'No,' he said. 'Go back to your position.'

And as he walked away, the collar of his coat pulled up against the early morning chill, he thought, but did not say: *Nobody can do anything for the poor souls down there now. It's the living who need our help.*

2

ADVANCE/RETREAT

On a bleak, remote island somewhere off the northern coast of Scotland, a lesson was taking place. The pupil was no longer a boy, but not yet a man. He had an adult's responsibilities, however. Some days they weighed more heavily on his shoulders than others. Today was one of those days.

Zak Darke's body ached. As Amelia Howard had been making her final journey from Brixton tube station, and most other boys his age had been drowsily hoping for a few more minutes' sleep before school, Zak had been starting his punishing daily workout. After that kind of beasting, most people would take the day off. Not Zak. His day was only just beginning.

The room in which the lesson was taking place was on the ground floor of St Peter's House, the desolate stone mansion that the boy had come to think of as home. There was a circular oak table in the middle of the room, and floor-to-ceiling windows that looked out over a windswept land-scape towards a choppy grey ocean. Zak stood at the window, staring out to sea. Unlike most students, whose distant gazes meant they were bored, Zak was deep in thought as he watched the rain whipping the remote island of St Peter's Crag. It was the middle of June, but the seasons meant nothing here. It seemed to rain all the time. There were no other pupils in this classroom, but there were two teachers: a young woman with white-blonde, shoulder-length hair, and a rugged-looking man, also blond and with a plain, square face and a flat nose. Since the death of Zak's parents in Africa – innocent victims of a vicious drugs magnate – and his recruitment as an agent, Gabs and Raf, Zak's Guardian Angels, had become his instructors, protectors and family all rolled into one. They both sat at the oak table.

'Nice hairpin,' Zak said to Gabs as he wandered back to the table.

Gabs's fingers reached up to touch the pin clipped to her hair. It was the size of a fifty-pence coin and fashioned in the shape of a star. 'Flattery will get you everywhere, sweetie,' she said, a flicker of pleasure crossing her lips. 'But how about we stay focused on our lesson, hey?'

Zak inclined his head. 'I still don't get it,' he said. 'How could they just let people die?'

'Because sometimes in war you have to make difficult decisions,' said Raf with a shrug. 'Don't tell me that's news to you.'

'I've never been in a war.' Zak knew he sounded grumpy, but he couldn't help it. This particular lesson was leaving a bad taste in his mouth.

Gabs gave him a gentle smile. 'Wrong, Zak,' she said. 'You've just never been in the army. People like us are at war all the time. Nobody reads about it in the newspapers, but that doesn't mean it isn't happening.'

Zak sighed, stood up and started pacing around the room. 'So let me get this straight,' he said. 'It's the Second World War and the Germans have a secret code called Enigma that the British have managed to crack. British Intelligence intercepts a message stating that the Germans are about to bomb Coventry. If they evacuate the city, the Germans will realize they've cracked the Enigma, so they allow the bombing to go ahead and hundreds of people to die.'

'In a nutshell, yes,' said Raf.

Zak shook his head. 'It's wrong,' he stated.

'It saved lives in the long run. If the Germans had

worked out that the British had cracked the Enigma code, we'd probably have lost the war.'

'It's still wrong.'

'Maybe we should just move on,' Gabs suggested. 'Nobody really knows if that story's true, anyway. Raf was only telling you to illustrate a point.'

'What point?'

'That codes are important. Governments and intelligence agencies spend millions every year on encryption and decryption software more advanced than a human mind could ever hope to achieve. Phone calls across the Atlantic are constantly monitored for trigger words. And, of course, the same goes for emails. To avoid it, you need very advanced encryption. When you're in the field, though, you're unlikely to have access to that kind of technology. You need to know how to send messages safely, and have a fighting chance of decoding enemy communications if need be.'

Zak nodded. He was feeling cross with his Guardian Angels, but he didn't know why. It wasn't like the bombing of Coventry more than seventy years ago was their fault, but he couldn't help wondering whether they – or their handler Michael, whose office this was but who never seemed to appear unless he had a job for Zak – would consider *him* dispensable if it meant saving others. Michael viewed the world a bit differently to most people, after all.

Zak put the thought from his mind. He was being childish. Not for the first time, he reminded himself that he had chosen this life. Just like the other young agents, one of whom he had already met in the field, had. Nobody had forced any of them into it. Though, he mused, it was hard to leave once in. Apart from anything else, he was officially dead, buried in a cemetery in north London, where he had once lived.

'With all that in mind, I'm now going to teach you a perfect cipher,' Gabs said. 'Easy to use, impossible to crack, even with infinite computing power.'

Zak gave Gabs a sceptical look. They had already spent the previous day working on codes – everything from Morse codes to written substitution codes or number codes. Why would this be any different?

'That doesn't sound very likely to me, Gabs,' he said as he retook his place at the table. He knew something about computers too; he had faith in their abilities.

There was a piece of blank paper on the table, and a pencil. Gabs started to write with a twinkle in her eye. 'Trust me,' she said. 'This method is called the one-time pad. It was used by the Special Operations Executive during the Second World War

23

and any sensitive military unit will be trained in some form of this. It's been mathematically proven to be unbreakable so long as you use it correctly.' She continued scribbling for a minute, then passed the sheet of paper over to Zak. Along the top of the paper, Gabs had written the alphabet, with a number below each letter.

A B C D E F G H I J K L M N O P Q R S T U
0 1 2 3 4 5 6 7 8 9 10 11 12 13 14 15 16 17 18 19 20
V W X Y Z
21 22 23 24 25

Below this, she had written what looked like random groups of letters:

J E H F Y J D

'Each number represents a letter, OK?'
Zak nodded.
'The random letters below – the line beginning with a "J" – are the key, and it has to be as long as, or longer than, the message you want to send. The person writing the code and the person deciphering it need this key. Let's say we want to send an order to advance. First of all, you write the message directly underneath the code.'

J E H F Y J D

A D V A N C E

'Then you convert the letters to numbers and add them up. If the number you get is more than twenty-five, you count from zero again. See? The third letter is seven plus twenty-one, which equals twenty-eight: that's twenty-five plus the zero plus two. So the decoded number to turn into a letter is a two.'

J E H F Y J D
9 4 7 5 24 9 3

A D V A N C E
0 3 21 0 13 2 4

9 7 2 5 11 11 7

'Finally, convert these final numbers back into letters.' Gabs did this and wrote them down.

J H C F L L H

'So, using the random key JEHFYJD, the word ADVANCE becomes JHCFLLH. To decipher it, you simply need to do the same thing in reverse – convert the coded message and the cipher to numbers and *subtract* the cipher number from the message number. Don't forget to include the zero if the top number needs to be increased by twenty-five. Look at the third number again. Two minus seven. Add the twenty-five and the zero – that's twenty-six numbers in total – to the two and you get twenty-eight minus seven. Twenty-one. V. Got it?'

Zak stared at the numbers and letters on the page. It seemed too straightforward to be unbreakable.

It was almost like Gabs was reading his mind. 'Most letter-based ciphers can be broken because we know how often certain letters appear in the English language. The beauty of the one-time pad is that the same letter in the original message can become different letters when it's enciphered. Look – the word ADVANCE has two As in it – the first one has become a J, the second one has become an F.' Gabs's eyes twinkled. 'I once told a boy I'd go out with him if he cracked a code I'd written with a one-time pad. He thought he was a bit of a brainbox, see. Bit unfair, really, with it being impossible and all, but I didn't really fancy him anyway.' She winked at Zak.

'So,' she continued, 'the killer feature of the one-time pad is that any letter can be turned into any other, depending on the key, which makes it impossible for the enemy to guess what you're saying. Try deciphering our encoded message of the word ADVANCE – JHCFLLH – using this random key instead.' Gabs handed him a piece of paper with the following letters: SDJOHLO

Zak carefully deciphered the original code using this new key. To his surprise, it revealed a very different message: RETREAT.

Gabs smiled at his obvious astonishment. 'It's not perfect, of course,' she said. 'You can only use the cipher key once, and because it has to be a long, random string of letters, it's practically impossible to remember so both people using it have to write it down. But as long as the key doesn't fall into enemy hands, the one-time pad is completely secure.'

Zak took a few moments to absorb all of that, then he looked up at Gabs and grinned. 'Nice,' he said.

'The one-time pad is unbreakable, but awkward to use. There are other similar methods we'll teach you that sacrifice a little security for a lot of convenience, but the important thing to remember is this: don't get so blinded by technology that you forget the simpler ways of doing things. Sometimes they're the best.'

'And it's sobering to think,' Raf added, 'that if the Germans had used one-time pads instead of Enigma, it might not just have been Coventry that fell, but Britain too.'

'Sobering indeed,' a new voice announced.

Zak looked around sharply. The new voice had no body, and it seemed to echo slightly around the room.

'I'm glad to see that Gabriella and Raphael are not neglecting your history tuition. The past can tell us a great deal about the future, Zak. We're in a privileged position, if we can learn from other people's mistakes. That's a charming hairpin, if I may say so, Gabriella.'

Zak realized that the new voice came from circular speakers embedded in the ceiling, and he recognized it as belonging to Michael, the mysterious old man who had recruited him in the first place and who controlled the missions he was sent on. He noticed that Raf's and Gabs's faces instantly grew sharp. Gabs stood up, walked towards the door and flicked a switch on the wall. A hatch in the ceiling that Zak had never noticed before opened up, and a screen descended silently along the oak-panelled wall opposite the windows. Michael was on-camera, sitting behind an empty glass desk in front of a bare beige wall, with no clue as to where he was in reality. Zak had no idea where his handler went when he wasn't here on St Peter's Crag; he was pretty sure that Michael intended to keep it that way.

'Your studies are going well?' Michael asked.

Zak nodded.

If Michael noticed that he was quieter than normal, he didn't mention it. He just smiled again before continuing to speak. 'I wonder if I might ask you to switch on the television?' he said. It was framed as a polite question, but of course it was anything but.

The TV was in the corner of the room. It was almost never switched on, but now Raf strode over, pressed a button on the side and it flickered into life. And for the next couple of minutes, the sound of the television filled the room, and silenced its occupants.

'*You join us at the scene of the devastating blast at Pimlico underground station.*' The young news reporter was slightly wild in the eyes, and breathless. '*Rescue workers are still trying to gain access to the platform where it is thought that an explosive device was triggered by the arrival of the first train, a little before six o'clock this morning. As yet, no contact has been made with the driver or any of the passengers. It appears unlikely, however, that there are any survivors.*'

The camera panned round to a scene of absolute

confusion. The whole area was cordoned off and there were countless emergency vehicles. Zak caught sight of grim-faced men in yellow hard hats disappearing down the underpass that led into the station, and a crowd of anxious onlookers had congregated nearby, some of them weeping.

'My information is a little more up-to-date than our delightful correspondent's,' Michael said. 'I think we've seen enough, Raf?'

Raf switched off the TV, and they all looked back up to the screen that showed Michael's face.

'My sources tell me that the arrival of the first Victoria Line train into Pimlico triggered the detonation of approximately twenty-five kilograms of C4 plastic explosive.'

Gabs gave a low whistle.

'My thoughts exactly, Gabriella. If there are any survivors, it will be nothing short of a miracle.'

The screen flickered. Michael disappeared and was replaced by some grainy camera footage. It took a moment for Zak to realize that he was looking at CCTV footage of Pimlico Station. The time code at the bottom of the screen told him that the footage was taken at 0231hrs. The platform was empty.

The screen juddered. Zak immediately noticed that the timecode had changed to 0145hrs.

'Hey, what just happened?'

'Oldest trick in the book,' Gabs murmured. 'Record some innocent CCTV footage, then super-impose it over the live feed when you want to camouflage yourself. Chances of someone noticing are tiny.' She raised her voice and addressed Michael. 'I take it, then, that the device was planted between 0145 hours and 0230 hours? Forty-five minutes isn't long for a job like that. Whoever it was *really* knew what they were doing.'

'My thoughts precisely,' Michael's voice replied. 'But there's more. We had a tip-off approximately five hours before the blast that this would happen.'

'Who from?' Raf asked.

The image on the screen changed for a second time. A photograph of a boy about Zak's own age. He had a thin face, greasy brown hair and a protruding Adam's apple. His glasses had brown frames and the lenses were so strong that they distorted his eyes slightly. There was wispy hair on his upper lip – he needed to shave, but had clearly never done so. He didn't look like someone you'd want to spend a lot of time with.

'Meet Malcolm Mann,' Michael said. 'Manny to his friends, although I'm reliably informed he doesn't have many of those. Certainly not in his current place of residence – Harrington Secure Hospital in South London.'

Michael appeared on the screen again. 'Young Malcolm is a remarkable individual.' He coughed apologetically. 'More remarkable than he looks. Six months ago, in one day, he successfully broke into the securest sections of the CIA, Pentagon and Department of Defense intranets. He did it securely – so securely that nobody would ever have traced it back to him if he hadn't boasted about what he'd done on his personal blog. Needless to say, all traces of his actions have now been removed and classified under the Official Secrets Act – no press reports. That would have been *most* damaging to the security of our two nations.'

'Why would he boast about it online?' Zak asked.

'You can read the psychiatric evaluations if you need to. The bottom line is that he's different to most people. Different, but brilliant. Socially awkward, but with a mind like a computer. Astonishing powers of analysis, able to see patterns where nobody else can. However, our American cousins would like his head on a plate. They want to make an example of him, you see, to put him on trial for breaching their security. It's all rather foolish, of course. If I was them, I'd be offering him a job.' He looked thoughtful. 'As a matter of fact, I still might.'

Zak ignored that. He was still catching up with what Michael had told him. 'Is he crazy?' he asked.

'No,' Michael said. 'Unusual, but not unstable.'

'Then what's he doing in a secure hospital?'

'The British government had him sectioned under the Mental Health Act. Rather a good idea actually, coming from them. So long as he's certified insane, they can refuse to extradite him. Malcolm, alas, fails to see it that way. Admittedly, he doesn't appreciate the full situation. He believes the authorities really *do* think he's mentally disturbed.'

Zak stared at his handler. 'That's horrible,' he whispered.

Michael raised an eyebrow. 'Really?' he asked. 'He's safe where he is, and can be looked after. Do you really think he'd receive the same level of care in a Federal jail – if the Americans even let him survive the extradition process? Or at the hands of the Chinese?'

'The Chinese?'

'Certainly. A computer hacker who is able to access the deepest secrets of American intelligence would be quite an asset, wouldn't you say? We know for a fact that the Chinese are interested in Malcolm Mann. The Iranians too, as it happens. Believe me, he doesn't understand the danger he's in, or that for the moment his accommodation at Harrington is the safest place for him to be. Of course, it isn't all charity. There are certain sectors within MI6 that would give their eyes and teeth to have Malcolm's technical ability. He's puzzle-mad, this lad. If he can't get his hands on a computer, he'll tackle anything – Sudokus, crosswords, logic puzzles . . . But now he's been supplied with a computer and an Internet connection in the hope that his keystrokes can be logged. He has, alas, found his way round this. We're none the wiser as to his methods.

'The Americans have agents posted around the institution. We know they're there; they know we know they're there. So far they've not been so bold as to try to kidnap him, but if we move him, they'll know about it. It would cause a diplomatic incident, bring the politicians on board. Nobody wants that.'

There was a pause while Zak tried to get his head around this information. 'Does *he* think he's mad?' he asked finally.

'"Mad" isn't really the word people use, Zak.'

'You know what I mean.'

Another pause. 'No,' Michael said finally. 'But, of course, nor do many people in such places, so he does rather fit in.'

'I still don't see what all this has to do with a bomb on the underground.'

'Patience, Zak,' Michael said in a low voice. 'I'm coming to that.' He cleared his throat and appeared to be collecting his thoughts. 'This morning, at approximately 0100 hours, Malcolm asked to speak to his psychiatrist. In all the time he has been in the institution he hasn't spoken once to an adult. Yesterday morning, he told his psychiatrist that there would be a terrorist attack at Pimlico Station very soon. Given Malcolm's rather curious history, the psychiatrist immediately reported it. It was, as you've seen, ignored by the powers that be.'

In his mind, Zak saw an image of a burning, mangled tube train and its burning, mangled passengers . . .

'Why did they ignore it?' he asked.

Michael shrugged. 'The authorities receive tip-offs galore, most of them from cranks and time-wasters. It's normally the case that genuine tip-offs can be confirmed by more than one source. That's the way intelligence gathering works. There was no real reason to believe that young Michael was doing anything other than trying to get attention.'

'How did the kid know about the bomb?' Raf asked.

'We don't know,' Michael replied. 'He won't tell us. Like I say, he refuses to speak to adults. He believes he's been poorly treated by them.'

'He's right,' Zak muttered.

'Possibly,' Michael said.

'Has he broken into the Americans' systems again?'

Raf cut in. 'Is that where he got the intel?'

'It's a possibility we should keep in mind. All he will say is this: that he will reveal his source when he's released from the hospital. This is what the government intend to do. I disagree with the decision. Our security services are not as secure as they think they are. That's one of the reasons we exist as an organization. If Malcolm Mann is released, I believe he will be in danger of assassination by the Americans or abduction by just about any other foreign power you care to name. And there are better ways of extracting information from people.'

'You don't mean torture?' The words burst out of Zak.

'Please, Zak. I'm not a barbarian. I would only condone that in the most extreme circumstances. No, it is the duty of *our* agency to do something a little cleverer, even if we are doing so behind the back of a blundering government. Which is where *you* come in.'

Zak looked at Raf and Gabs; they were already staring directly at him.

'You're going to break him out of the hospital,' Michael said. 'We'll plant the idea in the government's head that the Americans did it, and in the Americans' heads that the Chinese did it. While they're all shouting at each other, we can concentrate on the important business of finding out exactly how he came by this information.'

'Why me?'

'It strikes me, Zak, that you've asked that question before.' There was a pause. 'It has to be you because Malcolm doesn't respond to adults. We're gambling that he'll follow someone his own age, so long as you play it right. And, of course, can avoid any . . . compromising situations with any agents from other countries who may be watching our young Malcolm.'

'By play it right, you mean . . .' Zak knew Michael well enough by now to realize that he would most likely already have a strategy.

'I suggest lying to him,' his handler said bluntly. 'I want you to tell him that you're his only way out of there. That you work for a government agency that makes use of young people like him, and that you're the living proof. Be very persuasive, Zak. We need every last bit of information he can give you. Lives could depend on it.'

'And when he's told me everything? What then?'

'Then we'll inform the government that we've managed to locate him, extracted what information from him that we need, and put him straight back where he came from.'

'For his own good?'

'For his own good.'

Zak sat very still. He didn't know why, but he had an urge not to let any emotion show on his face. Not that he didn't feel it. Half of him was shocked at Michael's callousness, that he would let this boy rot in an institution and not even tell him why. The other half was excited. No other word for it. His mouth was suddenly dry with anticipation, his heart beating slightly faster. In a corner of his mind he wondered if it would always be like this, every time he was sent out on a job. He hoped so. Being stuck here on St Peter's Crag with Gabs and Raf had its advantages, but it was a lonely way to live. He realized that, after two major operations, one in Mexico and one on the high seas, he missed the thrill of being out in the field – of putting all his expertise into action, even if it was dangerous. It crossed his mind that Michael was shaping him to be that way, but he dismissed that thought almost immediately.

'When do I leave?' he asked.

Michael gave him a satisfied smile. 'Now,' he said. 'The government plan to release Malcolm Mann tomorrow. That means we have to get him out tonight.'

3

GREEN LIGHT

London. The same day. 1545hrs

It never failed to amaze Zak how quickly his surroundings could change. This morning he had been on the lonely island of St Peter's Crag. By mid-afternoon a helicopter containing him, Gabs and Raf was touching down on a helipad at the top of a tall building in Canary Wharf.

Zak wore aviator shades, a grey, oversized beanie hat and had a plain black rucksack slung over his shoulder. Flanked by Raf and Gabs, he descended to street level. Bankers in suits hurried by, mobiles pressed to their ears. There was a high police presence on the streets, and there was barely a pedestrian who didn't eye these uniformed officers nervously. But they were far too busy to notice the three of them climb into the back of an ordinary London black cab, its orange FOR HIRE sign extinguished. The driver barely acknowledged them. He certainly didn't speak as the cab glided away from the wharf into the centre of town. 'Only way to travel,' Gabs said with a half-smile. 'Nothing so ordinary as a black cab in London. Park anywhere, drive in bus lanes. MI5 have a whole fleet of them.' She nodded at the driver. 'And us too,' she said.

Zak knew London well, having lived in Camden with his cousin Ellie and his aunt and uncle, after the death of his parents. And he was also familiar with the apartment in Knightsbridge to which they drove. He'd been here once before, in advance of his first ever op. He remembered how on edge he'd been as he waited to take a flight to Mexico City, where his mission was to befriend Cruz Martinez, the son of South America's most notorious drug trafficker. He felt a pang of guilt. The last time Zak had seen Cruz was as he'd disappeared beneath the waves of the Atlantic Ocean.

Zak pushed the guilt from his mind. Cruz had brought his death on himself. He'd made his own choices.

Now, on his second visit to the apartment, Zak felt different. Nervous? Sure. But better prepared. More confident in his own abilities. In his own training.

The flat was luxurious – a snooker table, every games console under the sun, a fridge full of food in a kitchen bigger than most people's houses – but neither Zak nor his Guardian Angels were interested in any of that. They concentrated on the three brown parcels waiting for them on the kitchen table. Raf and Gabs took the parcels marked Agent 16 and Agent 17 respectively. Zak opened the parcel marked Agent 21.

It contained five objects.

The first looked like an ordinary hotel keycard. Zak knew, though, from his briefing with Michael, that it wasn't for an ordinary hotel. This was his ticket in and out of Harrington Secure Hospital. It would open every door he came across. At least, that was the idea.

The second object was a shiny new iPhone, pre-programmed with distress codes Zak hoped he wouldn't need, and with detailed electronic mapping of the hospital.

The third looked a little like an electric shaver, but with two metal prongs emerging from one end. This was a Taser. Powerful enough to stun but not kill. 'The hospital wardens patrol alone,' Michael had told him. 'There's never more than two at a time in the building itself.'

'Doesn't sound all that secure to me,' Zak had said.

'Don't get blasé, Agent 21. It only takes a single

person to raise the alarm. If anybody sees you, you need to put them out of action. And I can't emphasize enough how you need to be eyes on for any other interested parties in the vicinity. Remember, other agencies from outside the UK have young Malcolm in their sights, and we cannot afford to lose him.'

Item four: a wallet. It contained £200 in used notes, a credit card and a library card for Marylebone library. The library card had Zak's photo, but a different name. He had learned that names were like clothes – you wear whatever's most suitable for the job in hand. This particular name was a garment he'd worn before: Harry Gold. It was Harry who had travelled to Mexico. Harry who had befriended Cruz. Harry who had watched as Gabs gunned down his new friend's father, the man responsible for the death of Zak's parents. 'Hello, mate,' he murmured, before slipping the card back into the wallet and turning his attention to item five.

It was a weapon: a five-shot, 9mm Smith and Wesson snubnose revolver, housed in a neat leather ankle holster. Like Michael had said before they left, a secure hospital is exactly the kind of place you want to keep your firearm hidden in an unexpected location. If you came across an unstable inmate, you wouldn't want them to find your gun.

Raf and Gabs had no such worries. They would not be entering Harrington, so their parcels contained Browning semi-automatics, with extra magazines of 9mm rounds. For thirty seconds or so the silence in the apartment was broken only by the clicking and clunking of each of them carefully checking their weapons and making them safe. It wasn't until they were stowed away that Gabs spoke.

'Ready, sweetie?' she asked.

'Ready,' said Zak.

2357hrs

They had ditched the black cab. Now they sat in a black Honda CR-V in the darkness of the Cowper Lane Retail Park in South London. Zak had counted three other identical vehicles on the way here. True, they probably didn't have reinforced polycarbonate windows, enough to withstand all but the highest-impact rounds, but it was such a common make of vehicle that nobody would look at them twice. Perfect cover.

The retail park was deserted. PC World, Mothercare and Marks & Spencer were all closed at this time of night, and theirs was the only vehicle in the vast car park. The car park faced onto Cowper Road itself – a busy thoroughfare, but without any pedestrians as they were at least half a mile from the nearest residential area, pubs or restaurants.

Raf sat in the driving seat, his eyes switching between the side- and rear-view mirrors. Gabs sat in the back with Zak. 'Remember,' she breathed. 'Michael thinks the hospital could be being watched. We can't take the vehicle too close at this time of night – it'll attract attention. Don't lose your guard once you've extracted the target.'

Zak nodded. He had lost the shades and the beanie, and wore a black T-shirt and a pair of combats baggy enough to disguise the snubnose at his ankle.

'And, Zak,' Raf said. The blond man was looking at him in the rear-view mirror.

'Yeah?'

'I was watching you back on St Peter's Crag. You don't approve of Michael keeping this kid under lock and key. Fine. That's your choice. Just don't let it get in the way of your job. Don't do anything stupid.'

Zak sniffed, but didn't answer.

'He's right, sweetie,' Gabs said quietly.

Zak avoided her eye. Instead, he peered out of his window using a small, handheld scope to take in the surroundings and match them up to the maps of the area he'd already memorized on the chopper flight. The hospital was on the other side of Cowper Road, with another road called The Avenue running at ninety degrees to Cowper and along the eastern edge of the hospital. The hospital itself was surrounded first by its own car park, about the size of four or five tennis courts, and then by a wire fence about two metres high. He counted only seven vehicles parked on the hospital premises, but the barrier by the entrance was still manned – Zak focused in on a sturdy-looking man reading a newspaper in his little booth who would no doubt not even notice him if he walked along Cowper Road and turned right into The Avenue and along the eastern side of Harrington. Zak observed that the section of The Avenue that ran alongside the hospital was closed to road traffic – two wide orange barriers and a sign indicating that roadworks were about to start. He wondered if Michael had been pulling strings.

He double-checked that his keycard and phone were in his back pocket. Then he nodded at Gabs. 'I'm going in,' he said, and he stepped out of the vehicle.

It was a warm night, but very humid. A storm was coming. You could smell it in the air and almost immediately he left the vehicle, Zak heard a low rumble of thunder in distance. As he walked out of the retail park and left along Cowper Road, he came to a bus stop. A boy and a girl, both about sixteen, were snogging ferociously and clearly didn't even notice him as he passed. There was, so far as he could see, nobody else around – just cars and buses passing through. He kept his head down, and at the end of Cowper Road he crossed over and turned right, passing the orange barriers in the road itself.

He was on the eastern edge of Harrington Secure Hospital's car park now, walking alongside the high wire fence. On the opposite side of The Avenue was a children's playground – deserted, obviously – with common ground beyond it that disappeared into the night. The blackness unnerved Zak. It was like a cloak, hiding who knows what. He walked along the narrow pavement, keeping his head down. Only when he was adjacent to the hospital building itself did he stop.

The building was approximately twenty metres beyond the metal fence. From his rucksack, Zak took a pair of sturdy wire cutters and started cutting a small hole in the bottom of the fence. It took about thirty seconds to breach the perimeter. It crossed his mind that it had been rather easy and that anyone could easily do it, but then he reminded himself of something: the security here was to stop people getting *out*, not *in*.

He checked all around. No sign that anyone had seen him. And so he approached the building.

It was a bleak-looking place. Zak remembered the time his mum had taken him to hospital when he broke his arm falling from a tree. The memory gave him a pang – it seemed like a lifetime ago. But as he approached the grey walls of the building, for a second he was back at that hospital, crying as his mum tenderly squeezed his good hand.

Zak yanked himself back to the present. He was by a side door, sturdy and grey. There were bins outside it, which suggested to Zak that these were the kitchens. A good place to gain access at this time of night. Supper over, breakfast not for several hours. If anywhere was going to be deserted, it was here. To the side of the door was a keycard slot. It had a tiny red light above it, which flashed green as Zak inserted his card. The door clicked open and he was in.

The kitchens were dark. From his rucksack, Zak took a pencil-thin torch and switched it on. A beam of light – red, because that would preserve his night vision – cut through the darkness like a laser. As he moved it around the room it illuminated steel worktops and chiller cabinets. There was a strange smell – half disinfectant, half boiled vegetables. On the other side of the kitchen, ten metres away, was a second door, with the red glow of another key-card slot just to its right.

Zak strode across the kitchen, stowed his torch and slid the keycard into the slot.

Green light.

He gingerly opened the door and looked through. The dining hall beyond was also deserted. Even without the torch he could make out long lines of tables and another red glow on the other side of the room. Twenty seconds later he was pulling his Taser from the rucksack as he inserted his keycard.

Green light.

He winced. The empty corridor beyond was brightly lit. After approximately six metres, it turned to the left. Zak crept along the left-hand wall – being on the inside curve would give him a fraction of a second's advantage if anybody showed up. But nobody did. He passed four doors – two on the left, two on the right, all with keycard slots outside them. He knew from his examination of the schematics that these were patients' rooms. No noise came from them now, in the dead of night. He passed another door on his left that had no slot. He opened it to check and found himself in a linen cupboard, wooden shelves piled high with fresh sheets, a bucket and mop on the floor. Just as his schematic had shown. Good. He was following the right route. The ceiling was constructed of a grid of square plasterboard panels. Removable. A question flashed through Zak's mind: when had he become the kind of person who looked at a ceiling and saw an escape route, or a place to hide?

He was holding his breath now as he moved back into the corridor, his heart beating fast. It beat even faster when he heard footsteps.

He quickly backtracked and secreted himself in the linen cupboard where he pressed his ear against the door, and listened.

Nothing. A minute passed. Still clutching the Taser in one sweaty palm, he gently opened the door and stepped into the corridor.

'What the . . . *Who are you?*'

Zak's blood ran cold. He hadn't heard any footsteps because the hospital warden in his blue and white uniform was standing right outside the broom cupboard. He had obviously just rolled a cigarette, because he was tucking one behind his ear and holding a pouch of tobacco in his other hand. Zak didn't hesitate. He closed the couple of metres between him and the warden in less than a second, and pressed the Taser against his thigh. A shocking jolt passed through the man's body and Zak caught him under the arms as he collapsed to the floor. He was heavy, and it took all Zak's strength to drag him across the corridor and into the broom cupboard. He was sweating by the time he got the warden inside, but he didn't allow himself to relax once the door was shut. Instead, he fished into his rucksack and pulled out three sets of plasticuffs. First he bound the man's wrists, then his ankles. He added a gag made from a cleaning cloth, ensuring that the man would still be able to breathe, and finally he bound the man's wrists to his ankles so he couldn't stand up when he came round. That could be anything between one minute or twenty. Which meant Zak had to hurry.

He swiftly returned to his route: to the end of the corridor, then right. The door he wanted was the third on the left. He moved quickly but silently, remembering how Raf had taught him to tread lightly with the tips of his shoes before committing his whole foot to the ground. His hot sweat had turned cold. Clammy. He even shivered as he drew up outside the door marked with a number seven. This was it.

More footsteps at the end of the corridor. Then somebody cleared his throat. Zak slid his keycard into the slot.

Green light.

He opened the door and stepped inside.

4
ROOM 7

It was pitch black in room seven. Zak stood with his back against the wall and heard deep, regular breathing. That figured. Most normal people were fast asleep at this time of night.

Moving very slowly, so as not to make a noise that would wake Malcolm Mann up, Zak retrieved his torch. He covered the bulb with the palm of his hand, then slowly uncupped it to release the red light gradually into the room. He shone the beam to his left first. It hit the wall a couple of metres up. Zak blinked. Was it his imagination, or was the wall plastered with crossword puzzles? He followed the torch along the same wall. Nope. Not his imagination. There had to be a hundred crosswords, all pinned in a mish-mash pattern to the wall. He felt himself recording that little detail, like a camera was clicking in his mind.

He lowered his torch as it hit the back wall. The beam illuminated the centre of the room. A chair. A table. A laptop. Piles of newspapers and magazines.

He moved the beam to the right.

Eyes, staring back at him.

For the second time that night, his blood turned to ice. A figure was sitting in the darkness on the edge of a single bed. Motionless, like a corpse. But *not* a corpse. The eyes glowed red in the beam of the torch. They did not blink.

Zak's reactions were fast. He switched off the torch – it was like a beacon should the inhabitant of this room want to come at him – and took two paces to the left. He bent down and grabbed his snubnose from its ankle holster. Then he spoke in a whisper.

'Malcolm?'

'Are you here to kill me? Because if you're going to kill me, please do it quickly. A shot to the head should do it. I won't feel that.'

A pause.

'At least, I don't *think* I will.' The boy's voice had no emotion in it. He spoke at an ordinary volume that sounded excruciatingly loud to Zak.

'Why do you think I'm here to kill you?' Zak breathed.

The boy took a sharp intake of breath. 'You're not American?'

'Should I be?'

The shock of seeing the strange boy sitting there in the darkness, not to mention the strange conversation he was having, had confused Zak. He was half prepared to fight, but then some sixth sense told him that the boy hadn't moved, and that he was still just sitting there, staring. Zak turned the torch on again to see that he was right.

'You should go,' said the boy. 'They'll be here any minute.'

'Who?'

'They'll kill you too if they find you here. One down, two down, they don't care . . .'

It crossed Zak's mind that maybe this kid *wasn't* locked up in the wrong place after all. He felt his eyes narrowing in the darkness. 'Nobody's killing anybody,' he said, but he did feel himself grip the handle of his weapon just a little tighter.

'How old are you?'

'Fifteen. Listen, Malcolm, I work for a—'

'The *Daily Post*,' Malcolm interrupted.

'What?'

'Saw you looking. At the crosswords. Very clever. All the others think it's me being weird. Say I'm crazy. Don't get it, do they?'

Zak took a step towards him. Malcolm shrank back.

'I'm not going to hurt you,' Zak breathed. 'I don't think you're crazy. I'm here to help.' He held up his keycard. 'See this?' he said. 'It'll get us out of here. You and me. But we have to go now.'

Silence.

'Why?'

'Because otherwise they'll find me. The hospital staff.'

'I mean, why are you here to help? Nobody helps me.'

Zak glanced towards the door. He didn't have much time – the warden in the linen cupboard could start making a noise at any moment – but he sensed that this weird boy wasn't going anywhere without an explanation. Zak had his ready.

'Do you know why you're here?' he said.

'Nobody knows why I'm here.'

'I do. You broke into the Americans' computer systems . . .'

'It was easy, you know?' For the first time, Zak heard some emotion in the other boy's voice. It was almost like enthusiasm. 'I can do it from in here, even. I just—'

'And now various foreign powers are trying to abduct you,' Zak interrupted. Now wasn't the time for a lesson in computer hacking. 'You're being kept in here for your own protection. I work for a top-secret government agency. I'm supposed to tell you that they want to recruit you too. That isn't totally true. They might want to offer you a job, but more likely as soon as they've got what they want from you, they'll sling you straight back in here. I don't agree with that. But tell us how you knew about the bomb and I can help you later. If you *want* help, that is.'

Another silence.

'Yes,' the boy breathed.

Zak strode over to where the boy was sitting on the edge of his bed. He grabbed him by the upper arm, but he might as well have stuck his Taser against him since Malcolm shrank back at his touch. He clearly didn't much like human contact. Fine.

'Listen carefully,' Zak hissed. 'There are two guards. I've disabled one but he won't stay quiet for long.'

'What about the Americans? They *are* coming, you know. Tonight.' He glanced over at his laptop.

Zak chose his words carefully. 'We'll deal with the Americans when they turn up.' He made a point of not using the word 'if'. 'Now listen, when we leave your room—'

'Cell,' Malcolm corrected him.

'When we leave your *cell*, we need to hurry back to the kitchens. If we bump into anybody, let me deal with it.'

'Are you going to kill them?' Malcolm asked the question as if he was enquiring about the weather.

'Of course not.'

'It would be safer to kill them.' The boy felt in the darkness for his glasses and put them on.

'I've already told you: nobody's killing anybody. Just stick close, OK?' Zak saw the boy shrug his agreement in the darkness, then crept with him towards the door. He pressed his ear up against it. No sound, so he slipped the keycard into the slot inside the cell.

Green light.

Very slowly, he opened the door.

The corridor outside was deserted. Zak looked over his shoulder to nod at Malcolm. The boy looked thinner than he had on Michael's picture. Paler. The unshaved upper lip seemed more pronounced, but his eyes were sharp and wary behind the thick lenses.

'Let's go,' Zak breathed.

They ran down the corridor, Zak taking the lead and Malcolm following a metre behind. As they passed the linen cupboard, there was the muffled sound of grunting and thumping. The warden had clearly regained consciousness and was trying to get out. They ran on past, a little faster now, and their footsteps echoed off the concrete floor and walls of the hospital. Seconds later, Zak was letting them into the dark dining room. They were ten metres from the kitchen when Zak suddenly grabbed hold of Malcolm's arm again. Malcolm flinched, but clearly managed to control himself when he saw that Zak had one finger pressed up against his lips, and was now pointing in the direction of the kitchen door. There was a strip of bright light at the bottom. Zak had left it in darkness. It meant somebody was in there, and he was pretty sure they weren't making themselves a cup of cocoa.

Zak peered around in the darkness. To their left was a serving area – a series of hotplates with room behind them to hide. He jabbed one finger in that direction, and Malcolm appeared to get his meaning. He hurried over and hunkered down, out of sight. Zak himself returned to the door through which they'd just entered. He slipped his keycard into the slot, and as the light flickered green he opened the door wide, and left it open. As he headed back towards where Malcolm was hiding, he grabbed the end of one of the tables, lifted it up and then let it crash back down. The noise clattered around the room, excruciatingly loud in the silence.

Seconds later he was behind the serving area, crouching down with Malcolm. Zak was short of breath, but he noticed that Malcolm seemed perfectly calm.

It took twenty seconds for the kitchen door to open – Zak didn't have line of sight, but the light flooded into the dining room and he heard footsteps emerging from the kitchens. Two pairs.

Slowly – very, *very* slowly – he peered out from behind the hiding place.

He only caught a fleeting glance before the kitchen door shut, but it was enough to notice two things. Firstly, these were clearly not hospital wardens. They wore black jeans and black polo necks, not the blue and white uniform of the man Zak had disabled. Secondly, one of them at least – he had slicked-back hair and a flat nose – was carrying a firearm. Light reflected off the dull grey metal of a pistol that this intruder held by his side.

And then they were gone, having slipped through Zak's decoy open door.

He gave it ten seconds before nodding at Malcolm again. 'Let's go,' he breathed.

After crouching in the darkness, the brightly lit kitchen burned Zak's eyes. He didn't let that slow him down as he led Malcolm over to the door by which he had entered the building less than fifteen minutes ago. His mind was turning over as he slid the keycard into the slot. Who were the two armed men he had just seen? The Americans Malcolm had been expecting? If so, Michael had been right. Malcolm really *did* need protecting.

The rain had arrived by the time they stepped outside. Heavy, driving rain that reduced their effective visibility to about five metres. That was fine by Zak – it gave them extra cover – and it didn't seem to bother his strange companion either. He strode alongside Zak as calmly as if he was going for a country walk while they covered the twenty or so metres to the edge of the car park.

'How did you know?' Zak had to shout above the noise of the rain. 'That people were coming for you?'

Malcolm just gave him a sidelong glance.

'I saw footage of the bomb on the underground,' Zak persisted. He looked over his shoulder as he spoke, checking that nobody was following them. 'You do realize that we need to find the person who did that?'

Malcolm nodded matter-of-factly. 'They're cowards, aren't they, people who plant bombs? I don't like cowards.'

'So, you going to tell me what you know?' They were climbing through the perimeter fence now.

Malcolm started looking around as they reached the pavement. 'You said you'd help me hide,' he shouted. His glasses had misted up, and his hair was bedraggled. He was stepping backwards away from Zak.

Zak narrowed his eyes. 'Maybe you should think about that, Malcolm. If people really *are* trying to—'

He didn't finish.

So many things happened at once. Malcolm turned and ran. He had a lot of speed for such a slight frame, and managed to move a good five or six metres down the pavement before Zak could even make chase. As he ran after him, however, from the corner of his eye he saw something else – a figure on the opposite side of the road. He, or she, wore a black balaclava and leather jacket. But it wasn't the clothes that grabbed Zak's attention. It was the gun in the figure's outstretched arm, following Malcolm as he ran.

Zak increased his speed and dived at Malcolm, rugby-tackling him to the ground just as the sound of a gunshot rang through the noisy air. He knew from the sudden jolt of impact that Malcolm had been hit even before he saw the blood.

They hit the hard concrete of the pavement at the same time and Zak felt something splash in his face.

At first he thought he'd landed in a puddle, but then he realized the liquid was too warm for that. Too warm and too red. He looked over in the shooter's direction, but the faceless figure had disappeared.

Malcolm started to howl. His shirt was soaked red and Zak ripped the buttons open to reveal the boy's bony, bare chest. The round had entered between his left shoulder and pectoral muscle. By the look of things, it had hit an artery because blood was spurting out of him. The rain washed it away to reveal the entry wound, one centimetre in diameter. Zak felt for an exit wound on Malcolm's back. Nothing. The round must still be lodged in there.

With that level of blood loss, the screaming didn't last long. Ten seconds, max, before Malcolm's eyes started to roll. By now, Zak had pulled his phone from his pocket and punched in his distress code – six-four-eight-two. The enhanced GPS capability of the phone would guide Raf and Gabs directly to his position, but in the meantime, Zak had to concentrate on keeping the other boy alive.

The injury was catastrophic. Zak pressed hard on the wound, trying to stem it, but blood just flowed through his fingertips before being washed away by the torrential rain. He put two fingers to Malcolm's jugular, feeling for a pulse.

Nothing.

Zak's training kicked in immediately. In less than a second he was squeezing Malcolm's nose and administering rescue breaths. Two breaths in all, then Zak placed the heel of his right hand on Malcolm's ribcage and covered it with his left hand. Thirty chest compressions, short and sharp. Malcolm took a deep breath, and for a moment he almost looked conscious.

'Hold on!' Zak roared. 'Help's on its way.'

He heard sirens. As he bent down to perform two more rescue breaths, he was aware of activity in the hospital car park. Two police cars. More on the way, by the sound of it, and no prizes for guessing why. Zak cursed. He was supposed to be under the radar. Deniable. If anyone caught up with him, he'd have some explaining to do.

A vehicle crashed through the orange barriers that blocked off The Avenue. Raf and Gabs jumped out of their CR-V the second it came to a halt just a couple of metres away, half on, half off the pavement.

'What happened?' Gabs yelled.

'Gunshot . . . across the road . . .' He peered through the rain. Two figures were running towards them from the hospital. Thirty metres and closing. Zak could just see their faces. It was the armed men he'd seen in the hospital. 'Get him into the car!' he shouted at his Guardian Angels, even as he outstretched his right arm and took aim at the approaching figures.

Zak Darke had never killed a man before, and he didn't intend to start tonight. Instead, he aimed for the space between the two men's heads – they were running about a metre apart. The air displacement caused by a round passing so close to them would surely be enough to make them dive for cover. But Zak's aim would have to be good.

He squeezed the trigger. The stubby barrel of the snubnose sparked in the darkness, and the smell of cordite immediately entered his nostrils. Sure enough, the round missed both of the men, but was enough to send them to ground . . .

'*Zak! Get in!*'

Zak looked over his shoulder. He just had time to see Malcolm laid out on the back seat, Gabs tending to his wound, before Raf slammed the door shut and took his place behind the wheel. Zak sprinted round the front of the car to the passenger door just as a third gunshot rang out through the rain. The round hit Raf's side window with a dull thud, but wasn't enough to shatter the bulletproof glass. Even so, Zak had not yet even pulled the passenger door shut before the CR-V burned away, narrowly avoiding an oncoming police car, whose siren blared loudly before disappearing with a disorientating Doppler effect.

'What the *hell* happened?' Raf demanded as he drove.

'Malcolm tried to run. A gunman on the other side of the road put him down.'

'You should have been more careful.'

Zak let that pass. He turned to Gabs. 'Is he going to be OK?' he asked.

Her face and hands were smeared with Malcolm's blood, and she was too busy trying to keep him alive. 'He's trying to say something,' she said.

Sure enough, even though Malcolm's eyes were closed, Zak saw that his lips were moving. He strained his ears to hear what the wounded boy was trying to say. 'One down,' Malcolm whispered, a sinister echo of his words back in the cell. *One down, two down, they don't care . . .*

But then, an egg cupful of blood spewed from his lips. Malcolm fell silent, and Gabs continued the seemingly impossible business of trying to keep him alive.

16 JUNE

5

HIDDEN IN PLAIN SIGHT

They had gone from one hospital to another.

Zak had been here before. After his Mexico mission he had woken up here, and so hadn't known exactly where it was. Tonight he had been so distracted by the emergency in the back of the CR-V that he hadn't paid any attention to Raf's route until they reached Westminster Bridge. At the foot of Big Ben they had turned right onto Victoria Embankment and past the Ministry of Defence, before turning sharply left into an underground car park. Zak supposed he had passed this car park any number of times without really noticing it. Curiously, it contained no cars. At the far end, two large doors were flung wide open. Raf screeched up to them. The moment he came to a halt, Zak saw that six medics had surrounded the car. From that moment on, Malcolm was their responsibility. They had a stretcher waiting for him, and a saline drip, and a defibrillator . . .

Now they were sitting in a stark white corridor outside the operating theatre. 'Do you think he's going to be OK?' Zak asked for the third time.

With the exception of this repeated question, they had barely spoken since they arrived. Raf still appeared angry, and wouldn't catch Zak's eyes. Gabs, like Zak himself, was covered in Malcolm's blood. They looked like extras from a horror movie. The blood had dried into a sticky patina on Zak's own skin, but he didn't think about washing it off. There were too many other thoughts coursing through his brain. Not least that it could so easily have been two down, and not just one. Who had shot Malcolm? Was the gunman anything to do with the other two intruders? And how had Malcolm known to expect them in the first place?

'He's in the best place,' Gabs said. 'It's a private hospital. The security services use it when they can't risk patients being treated somewhere public. That's why you ended up here. They have the best surgeons. Trust me, if anyone can save him, these doctors can.' She didn't sound very convinced.

The door opened and a man entered. He was a good deal older than Gabs or Raf, had shoulder-length hair, bright green eyes and brought with him the smell of cherry tobacco. His face was grim.

'Michael,' Raf said. He didn't share Zak's momentary surprise at their handler's sudden appearance in the flesh.

There was no small talk. No 'hello's or 'how are you's. Michael got straight to the point. 'What happened?' he demanded.

Zak gave a precise account of his actions. He left nothing out. He'd been debriefed by Michael before, and he knew that the old man would spot any holes or inconsistencies in the story. Once he'd finished, Michael gave a curt nod and silence fell on the corridor once more.

'I don't understand how he knew someone was coming for him,' Zak said after a minute.

Michael sniffed. 'He broke into the Americans' systems once. There's no reason why he shouldn't do it again and find out whatever he wants. We gave him the internet-connected laptop in the hope that we could work out how he's doing it. He managed to bypass all our spyware and key-logging programs, of course. If I had to guess, I'd say the shooter was American. They'd probably prefer to talk to him, but in the absence of an agreement with us to send him over there, a dead Malcolm Mann solves a lot of their problems.'

'Do you think he found out about the Pimlico bomb using his hacking skills?' Raf asked. He sounded a little less surly now. Perhaps Zak's debrief had persuaded him that this whole mess wasn't somehow his protégé's fault.

'Undoubtedly,' Michael said. 'Our only hope now is to pray that he recovers enough to tell us what else he knows. Otherwise we're groping in the—'

'Wait,' Zak said.

The other three looked at him. He clenched his eyes shut, struggling as an idea formed in his head. He was remembering something Gabs had said to him only this morning.

Governments and intelligence agencies spend millions every year on encryption and decryption software more advanced than a human mind could ever hope to achieve. Telephone calls across the Atlantic are constantly monitored for trigger words. Same goes for emails . . .

He opened his eyes again. 'Sometimes the best place to hide is in plain sight, right?'

The others nodded.

'If you wanted to get a message to someone – say, where and when a bomb was going to go off – and you were worried about it being intercepted, you could try complicated encryption, or you could just put it somewhere nobody would ever think of looking.'

'Such as?' Michael asked. He had an intent look on his face.

Zak shrugged. 'I dunno,' he said. 'A newspaper crossword, maybe?'

Three sets of eyes stared at him.

'Go on, Zak,' Michael murmured.

'Malcolm had them pinned to his wall. He said that thing about other people ignoring them. I think . . . I think we should look at those crosswords. Say, for the last week. See if there's anything there. Any message.'

For a moment, Michael didn't reply. He glanced towards the door to the operating theatre. Zak felt Raf and Gabs's eyes on him. They were sceptical. But neither did they seem to have any better ideas.

Finally, Michael spoke. 'Do it,' he said. 'Malcolm will be safe here.'

With that, he walked down the corridor and disappeared.

You have a problem.

The words appeared in real time on the screen of a laptop. The man sitting at the laptop thought carefully for a few seconds before tapping out his reply.

I don't think so. Everything happened as I planned. You decoded my message?

He waited.

There is a hacker. His name is Malcolm Mann. My sources inside British Intelligence tell me he tipped them off about your first bomb. Luckily for you, he was ignored.

A link appeared on the screen. The man clicked it. It led him to a Press Association newswire. Shots reported outside Harrington Secure Hospital, South London.

Harrington Secure Hospital is Malcolm Mann's last known place of residence.

The man sucked on his teeth as he wondered how to reply: *Coincidence?*

Don't insult my intelligence. It's up to you, but if I was in your position I would want to be sure that nobody had solved your little puzzle.

The man felt his eyes narrowing. Perhaps his electronic pen pal had a point.

If the code had been cracked, there was only one place it would lead anybody. So he decided to watch that address. From the peg behind the door he removed a raincoat and a wide-brimmed hat. Then he left his simple apartment, making very sure to lock the door carefully behind him.

Back at the flat in Knightsbridge, Zak supposed he should sleep. It was five a.m. after all – almost dawn – and it had been, by anybody's standards, a long day.

But there was no chance of that. Not with a puzzle like this in front of him.

Once he and Gabs had showered off Malcolm's blood and changed into fresh clothes that were waiting for them, it had been a moment's work to download and print out the *Daily Post*'s crosswords for the past ten days. Raf and Gabs had humoured him for an hour by staring at them with blank faces. 'Sweetie,' Gabs had said just before they went to bed, 'I'm not sure this is time well spent.'

But Zak didn't agree. He had yesterday's crossword solution in front of him. He jabbed a finger at one of the solutions. 'Look,' he said. 'One down.' The word was BOMBING.

'That means nothing, Zak,' Gabs had said with one hand laid gently on his shoulder. 'It's just a word. Two down is OATMEAL. Are you telling me the next attack's going to be in a porridge factory?'

'Very funny.'

'Anyway,' Gabs continued, 'the bomb went off first thing in the morning, before anybody could even do the crossword.'

'No,' Zak objected. 'Don't you remember? Malcolm called his psychiatrist at 0100 hours. The early editions of these papers come out the night before. He could have seen the crossword online . . .'

Gabs had given him a slightly sympathetic look. 'You're tired, sweetie. We all are. Let's get some sleep, hey?'

Zak had rubbed his eyes. 'Sure,' he had said with a sigh. 'In a minute.' But a minute had turned into an hour, and an hour had turned into two. For all that time, Zak had stared at the crossword, somehow convinced he was on the edge of something, but not sure what.

Six o'clock came. Having stared at it for so long, he could see the crossword grid in his mind:

¹B	R	²O	G	³U	E	■	■	⁴A	B	⁵K	H	⁶A	S
O	■	A	■	K	■	⁷P	■	N	■	N	■	C	⁸I
⁹M	O	T	O	R	B	O	A	T	¹⁰I	N	T	R	O
B	■	M	■	■	W	■	■	■	F	■	I	■	D
¹¹I	T	E	M	I	S	E	¹²T	R	E	M	O	L	O
N	■	A	■	■	R	■	A	■	■	■	O	■	L
¹³G	A	L	E	I	■	■	¹⁴T	R	A	¹⁵I	P	S	E
■	■	■	■	A	■	¹⁶F	T	■	■	N	■	■	■
■	¹⁷B	¹⁸L	A	N	D	L	Y	■	¹⁹N	I	²⁰G	H	²¹T
²²U	■	E	■	■	E	■	²³A	■	O	■	A	■	H
²⁴D	R	A	C	²⁵H	M	A	²⁶V	I	V	A	L	D	I
D	■	D	■	O	■	■	I	■	A	■	L	■	R
²⁷E	J	E	C	T	²⁸R	E	A	C	T	I	O	N	S
R	■	R	■	E	■	■	N	■	O	■	W	■	T
■	²⁹A	S	Y	L	U	M	■	³⁰T	R	U	S	T	Y

Was there a sentence to be made up of these words? If there was, he couldn't see it. His mind focused on the word UKRAINIAN. Michael had talked about the Americans, the Chinese and the Iranians. Was there some other involvement? Was the word ASYLUM significant? It was, after all, an old-fashioned word for a secure hospital. He Googled some words he didn't know: ABKHAS, people who lived around the Black Sea; GALEI, a kind of shark. But no matter how long he stared at this puzzle, or at any of the others, no patterns or clues emerged. Gabs was right. He was following the wrong lead.

He stood up and walked across the room. There were large floor-to-ceiling windows here, looking out over London. The sun was rising and he could make out all the familiar landmarks: the BT tower, the London Eye, the Houses of Parliament, Buckingham Palace. From this high-up vantage point, he could see what looked like insects flying in the distance: military choppers, keeping watch over the capital. Zak wondered what they hoped to see. They were probably, he thought, just there to give the *impression* of security, when the truth was that London was very far from being secure.

When the truth was that London was under attack.

He thought back to the history lessons Raf and

Gabs had been giving him. When people imagined London under attack, they thought of the Blitz at the beginning of the Second World War. But times had changed. Enemies had changed. Now, they were more likely to plant a bomb underground than drop it from the skies. Malcolm had been right. It seemed more cowardly, somehow. And much, much harder to prevent.

His eye was drawn north to Camden, where he used to live and where his cousin, Ellie, still did – no thanks to Cruz Martinez, who had done everything in his power to kill her. She was only alive now thanks to Raf and Gabs. But she was alive, while Cruz was dead and his loathsome henchman Calaca was mouldering in prison.

His eyes picked out the area around Pimlico Station. From this distance there was no trace of the bombing . . .

He stopped.

Pimlico. Bombing.

Something twigged.

Zak hurried back to where he had been sitting. He double-checked something he was already sure of: the position of the word BOMBING in the crossword.

One down.

What if Malcolm hadn't been referring to his own

imminent demise, when he had whispered these words?

What if he had been giving them a message?

He grabbed a pencil and, on a sheet of scrap paper, wrote the two words, one on top of each other.

B O M B I N G
P I M L I C O

He cast his mind back to the lesson Gabs had given him just the previous day. The one-time pad. What if there was some kind of code, hidden here in plain sight? He scribbled down the alphabet, A–Z, with the numbers 0–25 underneath each letter in turn.

A B C D E F G H I J K L M N O P Q R S T U
0 1 2 3 4 5 6 7 8 9 10 11 12 13 14 15 16 17 18 19 20
V W X Y Z
21 22 23 24 25

It took him less than a minute to work out the key necessary to turn the word BOMBING into the word PIMLICO.

O U A K A P I

Zak stared at the cipher. Once again, Gabs's words rang in his mind. *The person writing the code and the person deciphering it need this key . . .*

He shook his head. He was still clutching at straws, trying to see something that wasn't there. Raf and Gabs were right. He should get some sleep. It felt like random strings of letters were dancing in front of his eyes.

Zak was about to push the crossword to one side when it jumped out at him. He blinked heavily and his mouth went dry with a sudden surge of excitement. He peered more closely at the grid and then, in a flurry of activity, scribbled out all the 'down' solutions after the first one.

OATMEAL
UKRAINIAN
ANT
KNIFE
ACTION
POWER
IODOL

And with a slightly trembling hand, he drew a circle around the first letters of these words.

O U A K A P I

The key. Hidden in plain sight. Both the code and the key in the same place. You only had to know how to look. Malcolm had seen it immediately – it was just the way his brain worked. And now so had Zak.

'Gabs!' he shouted at the top of his voice. 'Raf! Wake up! Now!'

They stared groggily at him. They hadn't taken too kindly to being woken, and they were clearly a bit confused.

'The crossword. It's a message and a cipher key all in one. Look.'

He showed them what he'd discovered.

'Michael told us that Malcolm sees patterns where nobody else can. It was obvious to him.'

His two Guardian Angels were looking at him with an awed expression. 'Very good, sweetie,' Gabs breathed. 'Our little cub is growing up.' She turned to Raf. 'I think we need to tell Michael, don't you?'

Raf nodded. He pulled out his phone and touched the screen, before stepping into the next room to make the call.

'Did you find anything else in the crossword?' Gabs asked. 'A time? A date?'

'The date the crossword appears could be the date of the bomb,' Raf called from the other room. 'Too

79

much of a coincidence otherwise. But could there be something about a time in there, Zak?'

Zak shook his head. 'I don't think so. But that doesn't mean there *isn't* anything else. It's just a matter of knowing where to look for it. There's something I don't understand, though. *Why?*'

'Why what?'

'If you're going to plant a bomb, why advertise it in such a weird way? I mean, either you want people to know about it, or you *don't*, right?'

Gabs nodded her agreement. The problem had clearly crossed her mind too. 'If you're going to do something like this, you're clearly not right in the head. Maybe the bomber's on some kind of crazy power trip. Maybe he gets a thrill out of knowing he's put the information out there in plain sight.'

'Yeah,' Zak replied. 'Maybe.' He wasn't convinced.

Raf returned. 'We're going straight to the horse's mouth.'

'What do you mean?' Zak asked.

'Somebody *set* this crossword,' Raf said. 'I think we ought to have a little word with them, don't you? Michael's sending me the details.' As Raf spoke, his phone buzzed. He checked the screen and nodded with satisfaction. 'A Mr Alan Hinton,' he

announced. 'Thirty-one St Mary's Crescent, Ealing.
Let's go. With a bit of luck we'll get to him before
he's even had his Weetabix.'

Raf gave a grim smile, and led them out of the
apartment.

6

THE PUZZLE MASTER

0638hrs

St Mary's Crescent was a pleasant, leafy street in a well-to-do residential area of west London. On the way, Gabs had read out information on their target that Michael had transmitted to her phone. 'Alan Michael Hinton, age fifty-three. Unmarried. No children. Writes crosswords, Sudokus, chess puzzles, that kind of thing – mostly for the *Daily Post* newspaper on a freelance basis. Uses the pseudonym "Puzzle Master". No criminal record. Not even a blip on the radar of the security services. Just about the last person on earth you'd expect to be involved in terrorist hit.'

'Either that,' Raf had said, 'or he's just got good cover.'

As they climbed out of the CR-V – Zak had sat awkwardly in the back seat to avoid getting stained again by Malcolm's blood – he counted three men in suits leaving their houses to go to work. They all carried colourful umbrellas against the pouring rain. A milk van trundled up the road, its glass bottles rattling. A bedraggled urban fox scuttled under a car. It was a very ordinary – if drenched – suburban street.

And number thirty-one was a very ordinary suburban house. A neat front garden with beige gravel and pot plants; a smartly painted red front door; a low brick boundary wall and an iron gate; all the curtains closed. The gate squeaked as Raf opened it and Zak followed him up the garden path to the door, while Gabs hurried off down the street, trying to gain access round the back.

It took Raf approximately thirty seconds to pick the lock on the front door using a set of standard lock picks and tension tools. Time enough for the rain to soak them through. Zak could tell instantly that something was wrong. As the door opened, he heard the scraping of mail against the floor on the other side. Either the Puzzle Master was extremely popular, or he hadn't been picking up his post. They closed the door behind them and took a moment for their eyes to adjust to the dim light.

The hallway led all the way along to a kitchen at the back of the house. A door to their left, a staircase straight ahead. And a strange smell. Very faint, but unpleasantly sweet. Zak had an uncomfortable feeling, and from the look on his face, so did Raf. Neither of them spoke. They just stepped forward to start searching the house.

The door on the left led into the front room. Wall-to-wall bookcases, stuffed full of hardback books and CDs of classical music. A TV in the corner, its standby light on. A very old three-piece suite with a floral pattern, and a russet carpet. But Zak had never seen such chaos. The floor was piled high with books and stacks of old newspapers and a coffee table was littered with perhaps fifty crosswords, all cut out from newspapers. It was incredibly dusty – thousands of dust particles danced in a shard of light that entered the room from a gap at the top of the closed curtains – and two large, black flies buzzed around the air. Occasionally they hit the mirror above the fireplace with a gentle thump, before returning to their aerial dance.

'Nice gaff,' Raf murmured, his voice dripping with sarcasm.

The kitchen was more sparse – and it gave the definite impression that the occupant of this house was not a keen cook. There was a dirty frying pan on the stove with a layer of congealed grease. Another fly was crawling on the white fat. A Yale key was sitting in the lock of the back door. When Zak saw Gabs appear, soaking wet, in the tiny rear garden, he unlocked it to let her in. Nobody spoke. Together, the three of them climbed the stairs.

As they approached the first floor, the sweet smell grew stronger. More unpleasant. Zak found himself covering his nose and throat, and he noticed the look Raf and Gabs exchanged.

'You should go back downstairs, sweetie,' Gabs said as they stood on the landing. But Zak shook his head. He could make his own decisions, and Gabs appeared to respect that. Zak peered into the small bathroom. A white bath with yellow stains, and a mildewing shower curtain hanging from a rail. A ring of stubble and shaving scum around the inside of the sink. The toilet seat was up, and it didn't smell too fresh. Zak noticed another fly buzzing around, at least as big as the two he'd seen downstairs. It was *only* a fly, but still: something about it made his flesh creep.

Zak froze. He could hear something. He looked up. There was a scratching sound above him. Movement above the bathroom ceiling. He looked over his shoulder at Raf and Gabs. They had noticed it too.

The scratching sound stopped. The only noise now was the buzzing of the fly.

There was a closed door at the end of the landing. Raf drew a gun as he approached it. Zak and Gabs followed a metre behind. The smell was now even more pungent, and Zak wasn't sure but he thought he could hear something else. A gentle hum. It came from behind the door.

A click. It was Raf releasing the safety catch on his pistol. He was a metre from the door and holding the gun out in front of him. He raised three fingers of his left hand.

Two.

One.

The force with which he kicked down the door was immense. It almost seemed to make the frame itself rattle. And as Raf burst into the room, something else burst out: a swarm of flies, perhaps several hundred of them, greasy and black, and a stench so bad it made Zak gag.

Through the open door, he could see Raf looking towards the ceiling. Zak stepped forward, waving his hand in front of his face to swat the flies, and hitting a couple of insects with each swipe. Gabs was close behind him, also gagging as they entered the room.

The air was thick with flies, all buzzing. The room itself contained nothing but a single bed and a bedside table with a glass of stale water beside it. Near the wall opposite the window, however, there was a trapdoor in the ceiling, with a loft ladder descending from it down to the ground. The flies were coming from up there, and so was the scurrying sound. Raf extracted a torch from inside his jacket and shone it through the opening and up into the loft. It lit up the soles of a pair of feet, seemingly suspended in midair to one side of the opening. It didn't take too much imagination to realize they were staring up at a hanged man.

'You don't have to look at this, sweetie,' Gabs said. Zak clenched his jaw and ignored her as Raf climbed the ladder. Then Gabs.

Then Zak.

He was sure, as he stared at the corpse, that he would not be able to stay there for very long. He had already seen two fat rats with long, scaly tails scurry away into the corner of the loft, and up here the flies were darting around so furiously that one hit his face every couple of seconds. The stink was putrid, but none of these were as bad as the sight of the body hanging from the central rafters high above. It was naked for a start. The skin was yellow and waxy, and it glistened in places where fluid had escaped. Rolls of fat seemed to have sunk from his torso to his belly, as though the skin were slipping down off his bones.

But his face was the worst.

The mouth and eyes were wide open, the nostrils flared. In the corner of the left eye Zak saw something move. It was, he realized, a maggot. More movement around the mouth. A scaly black cockroach crawled into the cavity, hiding from the light of Raf's torch. For the second time in as many minutes, Zak forced himself not to vomit.

'I don't know about you,' Raf breathed, 'but I don't think the Puzzle Master has set any puzzles for a good few days now.'

Neither Zak nor Gabs replied. They just hurried back down the loft ladder and returned to the ground floor where the smell was less malodorous, and they could at least breathe freely.

Back in the kitchen, Zak still felt nauseous and Raf opened the back door to let in some fresh air, and they all breathed deeply for a minute without speaking. Gabs broke the silence. 'Suicide?' she said.

Raf shook his head. 'I don't think he did it himself – there's nothing up there for him to leap from. No, the poor guy was killed.'

'How long has he been dead for, do you think?' Zak asked.

'Difficult to say. The roof wasn't insulated, so it could get pretty hot up there, accelerate the decomposition process. Even so, from the smell of him I'd say he's been there at least a week. A coroner will be more precise when they perform a postmortem.' He pulled his phone from his pocket. 'I need to report the death, update Michael.'

'We should search the place before any police or clean-up people get here,' Gabs said. 'See if anything shows up.'

Zak nodded. Together they went into the front room and started to turn it upside down.

At the end of St Mary's Crescent, a figure in a wide-brimmed hat and a heavy raincoat leaned against a pillar box. He had stood here watching as a black CR-V pulled up outside number thirty-one, and had counted three figures emerge from the vehicle. The rain was too heavy for him to make out their features clearly. Two of them were clearly adults, but could it really be the case that one of them was still only a youngster?

He allowed the intruders a few minutes to enter, then started to walk towards their vehicle. His right hand was in the pocket of his coat, and his fingers fiddled sweatily with a heavy, circular, metallic object. It was a magnet that provided the bulk of the object's weight. Remove that and the tiny battery-powered transmitter would barely register in the palm of his hands. Still, it was very powerful for such a small thing. There weren't many places on earth that the device's GPS capability wouldn't work, but he doubted that the people he was tracking would be taking a holiday under the thick canopy of the jungles of Belize, or underwater.

As he sidled up to the car, he wondered if they had found what they were looking for yet. He pictured them opening the bedroom door and looking upwards. Idly, he wondered if the corpse had decomposed enough for the body to separate from the head, or whether Mr Alan Hinton, the Puzzle Master, was still hanging intact from the rafters.

And as he walked round to the side of the car furthest from the pavement, bent down and slipped the magnetic tracking device onto the undercarriage, he found himself smiling grimly. Somebody may well have worked out his clever little code, but it didn't matter. He had other ways of getting his message out. Other ways that the right people would be watching.

That the right *person* would be watching.

The device clamped itself firmly to the undercarriage. The man crossed the road and continued walking through the rain to the opposite end of St Mary's Crescent. He didn't look back. He didn't need to. His job was done.

'I don't know how people can live like this,' Gabs

said as she flicked through a dusty pile of books on the armchair. 'This place can't have been cleaned for years.'

Zak nodded in agreement, but in truth his mind was elsewhere. 'Look at this,' he said.

In his hands he had a pale blue exercise book, like he used to write on at primary school. He had found it beneath a cushion on the sofa. It was mostly empty. Only the first couple of pages were filled with messy but compact handwriting.

'Listen,' he breathed, and he started to read.

Monday, 2 June
All the journalists I know say that when something strange happens you should take notes. So here goes. I had a phone call today. It was just before midnight. I was working on a puzzle. It was a man. His voice sounded strange. I saw a film once when the baddie used some contraption to disguise his voice. It sounded like that. I can't remember exactly what he said. I was too surprised, really. He asked me if I'd like to earn £1,000. 'Of course,' I said. 'You don't earn much writing puzzles,' I said. All I had to do, he told me, was replace three of my crosswords with three of his. Send them into the paper and make sure they were printed. I got spooked when he said that. I don't know why. I put the phone down straight away.

I'm writing this in the kitchen. I thought I saw something move in the garden just now. It was probably just a cat. Or a fox. They get everywhere. I locked the door just in case. I'll go to bed now. I hope he doesn't phone again.

Tuesday, 3 June
He called again today. Six o'clock, just as I was making my tea. I couldn't hear him at first because the sausages were spitting in the pan. He said he would pay me £5,000. I'm afraid I got rather angry with him. I told him to stop calling. He threatened me then. He said that he knew people at the paper, and could have me fired. I don't want to lose my job, but I hung up on him again. Did I do the right thing?

Thursday, 5 June
Should I go to the police? He's offered me more money. £10,000 to replace three crosswords with different ones of his own choosing. I said no, of course, and he got angry this time. Very angry. He said he would give me one more chance, and that I would regret it if I said no again.

I wish I knew who he was. Someone at the newspaper, I suspect. Ludgrove? I've met him a few times. He's a rotten apple. If only I could have heard the caller's voice properly, but he was still disguising it.

I'm frightened. I think I will go to the police. First thing tomorrow.

'That's his last entry,' Zak said quietly. 'I guess he was . . .' He looked meaningfully upwards.

Gabs stepped towards him and took the exercise book, her eyes lost in thought. 'Yeah,' she agreed with a nod. 'I guess he was. But before someone killed him, they got him to replace three crosswords. Not one. *Three.*'

'Three crosswords, three bombs . . .' Zak breathed.

'I think it might be time to buy a newspaper,' Gabs said.

7

THE SECOND BOMB

Zak still remembered the first time his mum had given him fifty pence to go to the shop by himself and buy some sweets. He'd been ten years old, and had run as fast as he could to the local newsagent, the coin gripped sweatily in his hand. But now he ran twice as fast, trying to find the nearest newsagent to the Puzzle Master's house. There was more at stake than a bar of chocolate.

Having turned left out of St Mary's Crescent, he saw a little parade of shops thirty metres down the road: a laundrette, an estate agent, a greengrocer and, to his relief, a newsagent. There was a queue in the shop, four men in suits clearly buying papers for their commute into work. A fifth man was at the newspaper shelves, about to help himself to the last copy of the *Daily Post*. Zak grabbed it instead.

'Hey, sunshine,' the man protested. Zak ignored him. He barged to the front of the queue, threw a ten-pound note onto the counter and, without waiting for the change, sprinted back out into the street and, barely catching his breath, returned to the Puzzle Master's house.

Raf and Gabs were waiting for him in the front room, anxious looks on their faces. There were a few more flies in here now, but Zak paid the insects no attention as he kneeled down at the coffee table, swiped a pile of books from it onto the floor and opened up the newspaper. The crossword – luckily not a cryptic one – was on the inside of the back page.

'You do it, Raf,' Gabs said, her voice tense. She handed him a pen and after about five minutes' concentration – and one or two Google searches for unusual words – Raf had the grid completed. Together they looked at the result:

Immediately, Zak's eyes fell upon the solution for one down. He felt a chill as he read the word 'explosion'. With a steady hand, he wrote it down on a blank area of the newspaper.

E X P L O S I O N

The word had nine letters. He quickly identified the next nine 'down' clues of the solution.

O S C A R
W H I N Y
Z E R O
H O O C H
I D E A
I D L E
D O G
P L O T
F O E S

His hand was shaking silently as he wrote down the first letter of each of these answers beneath the word 'explosion'.

E X P L O S I O N
O W Z H I I D P F

He glanced up at Gabs. 'Go on, sweetie,' she whispered.

Zak wrote out the alphabet, with a number underneath each letter.

A B C D E F G H I J K L M N O P Q R S T U
0 1 2 3 4 5 6 7 8 9 10 11 12 13 14 15 16 17 18 19 20
V W X Y Z
21 22 23 24 25

Then he filled the relevant numbers into his grid.

E	X	P	L	O	S	I	O	N
4	23	15	11	14	18	8	14	13

O	W	Z	H	I	D	P	F
14	22	25	7	8	8	3	15	5

With this done, he added the numbers together, starting back at zero for any result higher than 25, just like Gabs had taught him.

18   19   14   18   22   0   11   3   18

And finally, he wrote the corresponding letter beneath each number.

S T O S W A L D S

The three of them stared at the results.

'St Oswald's? That rings a bell,' said Raf.

Gabs, however, was standing up and pulling her phone out of her pocket. 'I'll Google it,' she said. She typed the word into her phone, then waited a moment for a page to load.

Her face turned white.

'What is it, Gabs?' Zak asked.

She was shaking her head. 'It can't be . . .'

Zak stood up, took the phone from her and looked at the screen. He read the first entry. It made his stomach twist.

St Oswald's Children's Hospital.

He tapped the link. The page took an excruciating ten seconds to load. A picture of a large glass-fronted building. Words beneath it, which Zak read out. '"Situated on the bank of the Thames, directly opposite the Houses of Parliament, St Oswald's Children's Hospital has been caring for sick children since—"'

He broke off. 'It's got to be a mistake. Nobody would attack a children's hospital. *Would* they?'

But Raf clearly thought they would. He was

already pulling out his own phone and dialling a number.

'Michael, it's me,' he said as soon as it was answered. 'We've got a problem. We're going to need a few extra hands . . .'

8

ST OSWALD'S

0726hrs

Mr Fraser Willis, of number 125 Leigh Avenue, Acton, had what most people would call a boring job. The job title had the word 'administrator' in it, after all. Fraser didn't care. Even though everybody saw him as a tedious pen-pusher, he knew that his job as hospital administrator at St Oswald's Children's Hospital was an important one. He wasn't a doctor or a nurse, but in his own small way he saved lives too, by keeping the hospital running smoothly on a day-to-day basis. Just so long as his job *remained* boring, it meant everything was going well.

When he emerged from the underground at seven o'clock that morning, the rain that had been falling when he left the house had stopped, and bright sunshine had taken its place. He smiled, but then saw that he had nine missed calls, all in the last minute. Something was very wrong.

Fraser was still staring at his phone when it rang again. Number unknown. He answered quickly. 'Fraser Willis.'

A sharp voice at the other end. 'Scotland Yard, anti-terrorist branch. What is your exact location?'

Fraser blinked. 'I, er, I've just come out of the tube station . . . Waterloo. Is there . . . is there a problem?'

'How long till you get to the hospital?'

'Four or five minutes . . .'

'Run. We'll have a team there in sixty seconds.' The phone went dead.

Fraser stared at it again, a sinking feeling in the pit of his stomach. Then he clutched the handle of his leather briefcase a little more firmly, and ran.

The hospital administrator was not built for speed. His legs and arms were thin and his suit flapped as he ran. By the time the huge glass frontage of the hospital appeared before him, his thinning red hair was damp with sweat. He stopped, wheezing, ten metres from the entrance. With the exception of a black Audi 6 parked up on the kerb, its hazard lights flashing, everything was as normal. He recognized one of the consultants walking into the building just as two members of the cleaning staff exited, looking tired after their early morning shift. It was only as he entered the building and looked towards the reception desk that he noticed anything different. There were two men he didn't know talking to the receptionist. As he entered, the receptionist pointed immediately in his direction. The two men looked round; a further two appeared as if from nowhere on either side of him.

'Fraser Willis?' asked one of them. He had short-cropped hair and a nose that looked as if it had been broken at least a couple of times.

'That's right . . .'

'You need to initiate emergency procedure 3A immediately.'

Fraser panicked for a moment. What was emergency procedure 3A? But before he could say anything else, the man was ushering him towards the others at the reception desk, talking quickly but under his breath so that nobody other than Fraser could hear. 'We have credible intelligence of an explosive device somewhere on the premises . . .'

'A bomb?' Fraser almost shouted. At a stern look from his companion, he lowered his voice. 'A *bomb*?'

'We have to evacuate the hospital as quickly and as quietly as possible. We have emergency vehicles on standby, but we can't risk making them too obvious too soon. The bomber could be watching the building, ready to detonate if he sees anything suspicious.'

Fraser wanted to run. He looked over his shoulder at the exit, but a firm grip from the anti-terrorist guy made it clear that his place was firmly *inside* the hospital.

They were at the reception desk now. Another of the four men – he wore a leather jacket and, Fraser noticed, a covert earpiece in his right ear – took over. 'How many patients do you have right now?'

'A hundred and thirty-eight,' Fraser replied automatically.

'How many can walk?'

'A . . . about half,' he stuttered. 'The remainder are bed-bound . . . very sick children . . . we'll need to move their beds into the lifts and—'

'Work from the top down,' the man in the leather jacket interrupted him. 'If the device goes off, the lifts will be out. I want the patients all congregating here in the reception area before it goes noisy outside . . .'

'Wait,' Fraser said. 'Are you saying the bomb could go off while everybody's still inside?' He spun round in panic, only to see that another four plainclothes officers were expertly dealing with any arriving hospital workers, most being shepherded

through the hospital towards another exit. 'It could
. . . it could kill *everyone*.'

The officer gave him a flat look. 'Then I'd say
we'd better get started. Wouldn't you?'

0735hrs

Jessica MacGregor was so tired that her body hurt.

The nurses had been kind, and set up a bed for
her in the room adjoining the isolation ward where
her little girl, Ruby, had spent the last forty-eight
hours. Poor, dear Ruby. She was only eight, but she'd
already had to deal with so much. The year of treat-
ment she'd had for her illness had been long and
painful. She had lost her hair, grown painfully thin
and seldom went a day without vomiting. She
always had a smile on her face, but her mother could
see through it. She knew it was put on for the
benefit of those around her. When Ruby was asleep,
the smile fell away, and so it was at night that her
mother couldn't help staring at her. It was then that
she was looking at the real Ruby. So poorly. Clinging
to life.

Jessica started. Two men had entered the room
and they appeared to be arguing. One of them was
Dr Khan, a kind Indian man who had cared for
Ruby so well. The other was a burly, broad-shoul-
dered man in a leather jacket. 'I'm afraid,' Dr Khan

was saying, 'this child absolutely must not be moved. Under no circumstances will I allow it. She is very weak and highly susceptible to infection.'

Jessica stared numbly at them. 'What's the matter?' she breathed.

Neither man answered her. 'Doctor Khan,' said the newcomer, 'this device could go off at any moment . . .'

'Device?' Jessica breathed. '*What* device?'

'What degree of certainty do you have of that?'

The man couldn't answer.

'If we move Ruby now, it is *probable* that she will not survive. Medicine is about the balance of risk, Officer. Ruby *cannot* leave the isolation ward unless she is wearing a protective suit.' He moved to the door leading to the ward and stood meaningfully in front of it. 'I will be staying with my patient.'

Jessica stood up. '*What . . . is . . . happening?*' she demanded.

The two men looked at her for the first time.

'Evacuation,' said the man in the leather jacket. 'Please proceed calmly and quietly to the lift.'

'I'm not going anywhere,' she said. 'Not without Ruby.'

The man looked at her for a brief moment. Then he spoke into a small microphone on his lapel. 'We need a protective suit. Isolation ward, fifth floor. Now.'

0742hrs

Fraser Willis wiped the sweat from his brow. 'No,' he told the three female hospital workers whose names he should know but didn't. 'It's not an exercise. We need all patients brought to reception on the ground floor . . . no, I'm not at liberty to say . . . yes, it is absolutely necessary . . .'

The fourth-floor corridor was bedlam. It didn't matter how calm anyone tried to be, moving twenty bedridden children, along with drip stands and oxygen canisters, was never going to be straight-forward. The younger kids were crying – thin, pitiful wails. The older children were looking anxiously at their nurses for confirmation that every-thing was OK, like nervous airplane passengers watching the cabin crew's faces during a period of turbulence. But the nurses looked as scared as the patients. Nobody knew what was going on. They just knew it was serious.

Fraser looked to his right. The area around the lift doors was congested – three hospital beds, clattering against each other like dodgem cars, pushed by hos-pital porters whose faces were sweating and whose eyes were slightly wild.

The crying continued. The air seemed stuffy. Fraser thought about his own son, no doubt just setting off for school.

He looked at his right hand and noticed it was shaking.

0756hrs

The wailing of the children had reached the reception area of the ground floor. Along with a little boy whose leg was in a cast, Fraser had emerged from the lift to a scene of chaos. He quickly counted up the number of beds down here. Forty-three. There was no room for any more. They were going to have to let the patients out onto the hospital forecourt. Fraser's mouth went dry. If he joined the children outside the hospital, where it was safe, would it be noticed? Would it be a dereliction of duty?

One of the anti-terrorist officers pushed past him. He was talking into his lapel. 'This is team Alpha Five. We've reached saturation point at the assembly area. We'll start bringing them out in sixty, six zero, seconds.'

Fraser looked towards the glass frontage. The crowd outside could see what was happening. It had tripled in size – maybe forty people now. If the bomber *was* watching, he or she would know something was going on.

He started edging through the sea of hospital beds and drip stands towards the exit.

'Willis!' A voice barked over the crying and the clattering. Fraser spun round. The officer in the leather jacket was beckoning to him, with a steely glint in his eye. 'Going somewhere?' he demanded.

Fraser shook his head.

'We're about to open up. It's going to get noisy outside. Emergency vehicles, bomb disposal.' He looked towards the ceiling. 'I need you on the upper floors, make sure everyone's evacuated. We've got a kid in the isolation ward on the fifth floor.'

'Ruby MacGregor.'

'Whatever. Mother won't leave her. Nor will the doctor. I've put a call out for a protective suit. Just so you know.'

Fraser swallowed hard. 'But if the bomber sees—' he started to say.

'We can only keep this cover for so long,' the officer interrupted.

'But what if he . . . what if he *detonates*?'

The officer blinked at him. 'Then we'll go to our graves knowing we did our best to save some sick kids from a sick terrorist. Right?'

Fraser swallowed hard again. His eyes flickered towards the exit, and then towards the lift. 'Right,' he said.

0757hrs

The CR-V containing Zak, Gabs and Raf approached the hospital at a steady speed. All the way here, Raf had been burning up the roads, running red lights, cutting up angry commuters, holding the steering wheel lightly but with a look of intense concentration on his face and beads of sweat on his forehead.

'What's happening?' Zak had demanded as soon as they'd sped off. Raf had spoken to Michael for no more than thirty seconds, and had been silent as he hit the accelerator. Zak had appealed to Gabs, who still hadn't regained her composure. 'What's _happening?_'

'Evacuation,' she'd said curtly. 'It's the only thing they can do.' She'd cursed under her breath. 'What sort of monster targets a children's hospital?'

It was a good question, but it wasn't the only one in Zak's sickened mind. What sort of monster targets a children's hospital, _and_ advertises it using some coded message?

'When we get there,' Raf had said finally, 'no heroics, OK?'

'What do you mean?'

'The guys evacuating the building will be professionals. Same goes for whoever's locating the device. They won't thank you for getting in their way.'

'What about you two?' Zak had demanded.

Raf and Gabs exchanged a glance. 'We're older, sweetie,' Gabs said. Her tone of voice indicated that this was her last word on the matter.

Having reached Lambeth Palace Road, they'd slowed down. 'What's wrong?' Zak had breathed.

'If they've got any sense,' Raf said, 'they'll be performing the first part of the evacuation covertly, gathering as many patients as they can near to the exit before extracting them. Just in case someone's watching.'

The building that Zak had seen on Gabs's phone came into view. It was about five storeys high, and encased in tinted glass that reflected the June sun. It was as if their arrival had triggered something. There was a sudden burst of activity at the front of the hospital. The doors opened, and the small crowd that had gathered parted as harassed-looking hospital staff wheeled out a hospital bed and a drip stand. Suddenly five emergency vehicles – three ambulances and two fire appliances – appeared from nowhere and pulled in front of the hospital. Their sirens were off, no lights were flashing. But in the distance Zak could hear the sound of more emergency vehicles approaching.

As the three of them jumped out and took a moment to check what was happening, he heard something else too: the now-familiar low chug of a chopper nearby. At first he couldn't see it; seconds later, it rose ominously from behind the hospital. The chopper skimmed over the top of the building, then started to descend nosily until it settled on the ground twenty metres from the entrance of the hospital. The downdraught was immensely strong, and everyone in the vicinity bowed their heads and covered their eyes. Zak watched breathlessly as the side door of the chopper opened, and two figures stepped out. Even above the noise of the rotor blades, he thought he heard someone scream at the sight of them.

They were indeed a scary vision, these two men in their green-brown blast suits and protective helmets, not a single inch of them exposed. They walked awkwardly in their heavy boots, like space-men on the moon, each carrying metal flight cases. Behind them, another man and a woman emerged from the helicopter, dressed in plainclothes and each holding two dogs on leads. German Shepherds, by the look of them. 'Bomb disposal unit!' Raf shouted above the noise. 'And sniffer dogs. Flown in from Wellington Barracks. The dogs are trained to sniff out explosives.'

More movement at the main entrance to the hospital. Soldiers in DPMs had appeared. They were carrying standard-issue SA80s and were barking at the onlookers to get away from the building. Two of them started erecting a cordon twenty metres from the hospital exit; others were shouting at the hospital workers not to loiter near the door but to get past the cordon. Zak's eyes were drawn to the children in the beds. They looked very young, very thin and very scared. One of them, a little girl with red hair and freckles, was sitting up and crying. Wailing for her mother.

'What kept you?'

Michael didn't even turn his head as he strode past them. His face was grim, his eyes tired, but he walked with the purpose of a man half his age. Without a word, they followed him to a white van, the rear doors of which were open and the inside filled with a bank of screens. Each screen showed an interior of the hospital in grainy black and white. Sitting in front of them, wearing a microphone, a headset and a furrowed brow, was a plainclothes surveillance operative. There were no introductions, but Zak wasn't expecting any. He turned his attention back to the screens. In one of them there were twenty or thirty occupied beds. Another looked down onto a corridor, where a hospital porter was pushing another bed in the direction of the lift. A third screen showed an empty ward where the curtains that once surrounded the beds flapped ominously.

'We have a feed into the hospital CCTV,' Michael said. 'Bomb-disposal personnel are going in now. They'll have robotic cameras, we'll have a feed into those too when they're operational.' He pinched the area between his eyes. 'But it's a big hospital,' he said. 'If we don't get it evacuated in time . . .' His voice trailed off.

'We should help with the evacuation,' Gabs said.

Michael and Raf nodded. 'Zak,' Raf said. 'Stay here.'

'I want to come. I can help.'

Gabs shook her head. 'No way, sweetie,' she said. She reached out and brushed his cheek with the back of her hand. 'You've done enough. Now you need to stay safe.'

'But—'

'It's an order,' Michael said abruptly. 'We don't have time to argue.' He looked at the other two. 'Let's go,' he said.

Seconds later, Zak was alone apart from the surveillance operator.

He paced the inside of the van impatiently. He felt useless, stuck there in the middle of it all and yet unable to do a thing.

'If you're going to pace, pace outside,' said the

surveillance guy. Zak cast him a black look, but the man wasn't paying any attention to him – he had eyes only for his screens. The noises outside continued to blare. Zak had heard the chopper rise off the ground, but it sounded like it was still circling above the hospital and he looked outside to check. There it was – a great black beast keeping watch over this chaotic scene.

The bomb-disposal guys were now heading into the hospital. The sniffer dogs were behind them, pulling frantically at their leads. They showed no sign of fear – the dogs were clearly well trained to deal with situations like this – and when their handlers let them go, they scampered into the entrance. The hospital staff were still wheeling out the beds of sick children. Zak looked around. To his west, the River Thames with the Houses of Parliament on the other side. Closer at hand, paramedics tending to the terrified young patients, and armed troops barking at members of the public to stay back.

Was the bomber watching, Zak wondered? Was he waiting for the moment to strike that would cause the most harm?

One of the soldiers caught his eye and gave him a confused look. Zak had no ID, nothing to say he was permitted inside the cordon, so he quickly stepped back into the van. Out of sight, out of mind. He hoped.

He looked at the screens. The images of the hospital's interior were sinister – being silent, they gave no soundtrack to the chaos within. Zak had a bizarre recollection of watching *Big Brother* on TV. While the contestants had been sleeping, the cameras had shown silent, empty corridors. The CCTV in the upper levels of the hospital looked similar, but every few seconds the screen was filled with a moving bed and drip stand or, on one occasion, a nurse carrying a small bundle that could only be a sick baby. Zak could barely watch. He turned his attention to one of the other screens.

'Dog's going crazy,' the surveillance guy said. He was right. One of the German Shepherds looked as though he was chasing his tail. 'Happens sometimes. They get spooked. They're trained to give certain signals if they find something, but that one's a waste of space. Dogs' home for him. What you doing here anyway, son?'

'Just along for the ride,' Zak breathed. He couldn't take his eyes off the German Shepherd. Something wasn't quite right. 'Where's that dog?'

'Ground floor,' said the surveillance guy. 'Corridor on the north side.'

'Can you zoom in on it?'

'What is this? Pets' corner?'

'*Can* you?'

The surveillance guy gave him a slightly confused look, then shrugged and turned a dial on the VT equipment in front of him. The CCTV camera focused in on the German Shepherd. Zak peered more closely at it. Even in this grainy image he could see that the dog's eyes were bright, its ears sharp. It stopped suddenly, and although Zak couldn't hear it, he could see the dog bark as its handler surveyed the area, clearly looking for a place where a bomb could be hidden. But it was just an area of open floor. The dog cocked its head, and for a moment seemed to look directly into the camera at Zak. But then it started chasing its tail again.

'That dog's not spooked,' Zak muttered, just as the handler gave a thumbs up to the CCTV and gestured the dog to move on.

'What you say, son?'

'That dog's not spooked. I'm sure he's found something.'

But the surveillance guy didn't hear any more of what Zak had said, because by the time Zak had finished speaking he'd already jumped out of the back of the van.

9

CASUALTY OF WAR

Zak needed to tell someone. Fast.

As he jumped back out onto the pavement, he scanned quickly around for Raf, Gabs or Michael. There was no sign of them. He ran in the direction of the hospital entrance, but he was fifteen metres away when he found his path blocked by a sturdy figure in DPMs carrying an SA80. Before he knew it, a steely-faced soldier was barking at him: '*Get back! Behind the cordon! Now!*'

Zak opened his mouth to argue, but he clamped it shut just as quickly. There was nothing he could say that would make the soldier believe he was supposed to be on site. That it was thanks to him all this was happening anyway. He held up his palms in surrender and stepped backwards. As soon as the soldier saw that Zak was retreating, he turned away.

Zak hurried back to the van, slipped behind it, waited a few seconds, and then approached the hospital from a different angle. He kept his head upright and his stride purposeful. He needed to look like he was supposed to be here. And, after all, everyone was being evacuated; the only people walking towards the scene were those with jobs to do.

There was an ambulance parked between the van and the hospital. Its rear doors were open and an empty stretcher bed was stationed just behind it. The paramedics from the ambulance itself were not there – presumably they were tending to the evacuated children whose beds were still crowded around the front of the hospital. Zak moved almost on instinct. He jumped into the back of the ambulance where he immediately located a high-visibility medic's jacket and a blue cloth surgeon's face mask. He quickly put them on, hoping that they would hide how young he looked, then exited the ambulance and pushed the empty stretcher bed in the direction of the hospital.

There was a parting in the middle of the sea of beds, a narrow path that led straight to the entrance of the hospital. Zak manoeuvred the stretcher bed along it, fully prepared to be challenged at any moment. But nobody did. Before he knew it, he was inside.

The reception area was not as full as it had been when Zak had looked at it on the monitor, but it was still chaotic. Red-faced soldiers were barking commands at scared-looking hospital staff; those few children whose beds remained here were still crying. Zak took a moment to get his bearings. Left was north. The surveillance guy had said that the sniffer dog had been on the ground floor. If Zak's instinct was right, that meant he had to get down to the basement. He looked over towards the lift. There was a set of double doors just to its right, and a blue sign saying 'Stairs'. Still pushing the stretcher bed, he headed towards them. He smashed the bed through the double doors and then, while they were still swinging shut, abandoned it and hurtled down the stairs three at a time.

Keep your bearings, he told himself. *Head north*.

Fraser Willis couldn't remember the last time he had cried. He was a grown man, after all. But he was on the edge of tears now. All he wanted to do was to get out of the hospital. To safety.

All he wanted to do was make sure that he didn't die.

Fraser would have run away already if it hadn't been for the anti-terrorist officer in the leather jacket. He always seemed to be there, keeping his steely eye on Fraser. He was bearing down on him now, as Fraser stood, sweaty-palmed, in the almost empty reception area with one eye on the exit.

'The kid in the isolation ward.' The officer started talking loudly before he had even reached Fraser. 'We've no isolation suits in the vicinity. What are our options?'

Fraser tried to clear the panic from his head. 'I . . . I may be able to find something,' he stuttered. 'There's a storeroom in the basement . . . perhaps . . .'

The officer's lip curled. 'Are you telling me,' he hissed, 'that you had an isolation suit here all the time?'

'I . . . I can't be sure . . . very confusing, all this . . .' He felt his eyes drawn once more to the exit.

The officer grabbed the frightened hospital administrator by the scruff of the neck. 'Find it,' he growled, before pushing him away.

Fraser almost fell. He scampered backwards, then scurried towards the double doors to the right of the lift. He ignored the stretcher bed that somebody had abandoned at the top of the stairs and hurried down into the basement of the hospital. He moved quickly, not because he feared for the life of little Ruby MacGregor on the fifth floor, but because he feared for his own.

*   *   *

Zak tried not to think of the weight of the hospital building above him, or of how totally he would be crushed if the device he was hunting detonated now. It wasn't easy. He passed two empty wards and a storeroom, all the while trying to work out his position in relation to where he had seen the dog chasing its tail. At the end of the corridor was a closed door. He burst through it and took a moment to look around. It was some kind of locker room. It reminded him a bit of the changing rooms at the swimming pool his mum and dad used to take him to – benches along the middle, with hooks above, and metal lockers along each wall. He presumed that this was where the hospital staff got changed.

Zak looked up. The ceiling was a grid of square plaster panels. Removable. For a moment he was back at Harrington Secure Hospital, hiding in a linen cupboard and wondering when he had become the sort of person who looked at a ceiling and saw an escape route, or a place to hide.

A place to hide . . .

He swallowed nervously and tried to rid himself of the cold sensation that ran through his veins. Then he stood on one of the benches, stretched up on tiptoes, and pushed gingerly at one of the panels.

It moved.

Zak edged the panel to the left so that a square opening appeared in the ceiling. He grabbed two edges of the opening and hauled himself up. The muscles in his upper arms burned, but he had enough strength from Raf and Gabs's intensive training regimes back on the island to pull himself up and into the ceiling. The cavity between the plaster panels and the underside of the floor was about a metre deep, which meant he had to stay in a crouching position. He was slightly out of breath now, but the pumping of his pulse was down to anxiety, not exertion. He blinked. He had fully expected it to be dark up here.

But it wasn't.

There was a blue glow. It was approximately ten metres away. Zak took a deep breath to calm himself, then carefully started crawling in the direction of the glow.

He had a good idea of what he was looking at by the time he was five metres away. But he crawled up close to the glow just to be sure.

It was a small digital display, half the size of a mobile phone. The blue glow came from the numbers on the display. They were counting down.

00:04:33
00:04:32
00:04:31

Zak stared at the display for a moment, almost paralysed with the shock of knowing he had found the detonator. His fingers edged towards the display, but they were a centimetre away when he stopped himself from touching it. He scrambled in his pocket for his mobile phone. With a couple of taps of the screen, he had turned the camera flash into a high-powered torch beam. He shone it at the display to reveal two wires leading from it. The display itself was balanced on a tiny see-saw mechanism, and there were wires leading from this too. Zak instantly saw that if he had touched it, he would have triggered the booby-trapped device.

Barely daring to move, he allowed the torch beam to follow one of the wires. It ran along the ceiling for a couple of metres before reaching a thick steel post, sturdy enough, Zak reckoned, to be part of the skeleton of the building. He followed the wire upwards. When the torch beam reached the underside of the ground floor, he stopped and, despite himself, drew a sharp intake of breath.

They were everywhere.

The cakes of plastic explosive were strapped to the underside of the ground floor with thick black gaffer tape. Each one was about twenty centimetres by twenty, and Zak couldn't even count them all – at a glance he estimated that there were more than fifty. No wonder the sniffer dog was going wild on the floor just above. Whoever had planted these explosives had concentrated on the area around the steel post, and another one a few metres beyond it. Zak was no engineer, but he could immediately tell why: bring down these weight-bearing structures, and you'd bring down the whole building.

His eyes flickered back to the detonator.

00:04:01
00:04:00
00:03:59

His limbs were like jelly as he backed away, terrified that the wrong movement would spring the booby trap. His body shrank away from the underside of the floor above him, and the moment he reached the opening he jumped back down into the locker room. He sprinted out of the room and back along the corridor.

It was just as he was passing the storeroom that the door opened and a man stepped out. He was wearing a crumpled suit and his thinning red hair was damp with sweat. He was carrying a package, but as Zak collided with him, he dropped it.

'Get out of the building!' Zak screamed at him. 'I've found the bomb. We've got less than four minutes.'

The man gave him a sickened look. Then he dropped the package and sprinted for the stairs, with Zak only metres behind him.

They burst through into the reception area. The red-haired man ran straight for the exit while Zak looked desperately around until his eyes fell on Gabs. She was on the opposite side of the room and was helping move what looked like the final patient out of the building. When she saw Zak her face darkened, but Zak ran towards her anyway.

'I've found it,' he said breathlessly. 'It's on a timer in the space between the basement ceiling and the first floor. Less than three minutes to go.'

No trace of panic crossed Gabs's face. She strode up to a plainclothes officer whose nose looked like it had been broken and spoke a few quiet words to him. The officer's face paled. He headed over to the reception desk, where he spoke into a microphone. His voice echoed around the hospital tannoy system. '*All emergency and non-emergency personnel to evacuate the building immediately. Repeat, all emergency and non-emergency personnel to evacuate the building immediately.'*

Chaos. Panic. A rush for the exit. All the patients, it seemed, had been extracted. The thirty or so people who started running into the reception area from other parts of the hospital were military, police, bomb-disposal and medical staff. They crowded round the exit, pushing against each other. Jostling. Gabs and Zak joined them. His Guardian Angel was giving him a strange look, clearly wondering how he'd found the device. But now wasn't the time to talk about it. Besides, something else had caught Zak's attention. Standing a couple of metres away were two men, one in a leather jacket, the other with the broken nose.

'What about the kid on the fifth-floor isolation unit?'

'Doctors wouldn't let us move her without a protective suit. Apparently she's on such strong drugs that any infection from elsewhere – picked up from anyone around her, even her own mother – could kill her. That wimp of an administrator went down to the basement to get one, but it's too late now.' The face of the man with the broken nose was grim. 'I guess the poor kid's going to be a casualty of war.'

The words of these men were like a knife in Zak's stomach. He turned to Gabs, who had obviously also overheard the conversation, and just as obviously felt the same way. He remembered the red-haired man and the package he'd dropped in the basement.

'I think I know where the protective suit is,' Zak stated.

Gabs nodded. 'Get it. I'll meet you on the fifth floor. Use the stairs.'

And with that, they were both sprinting from the exit towards the stairwell, where Gabs sprinted up and Zak descended once more into the bowels of the hospital.

In the dark cavity above the locker room, the small blue display continued to count down. It was only a machine, so it was oblivious to the destruction and human suffering it was about to cause.

. . . it read.

10

00:00:00

The protective suit was where the hospital administrator had dropped it. Zak scooped it up from the floor and sprinted back to the stairwell.

He felt sick at the thought of what he was doing as he lunged up the stairs, his lungs burning from exhaustion. He found it impossible to keep track of the time. How long until detonation? Two minutes? One minute? Less? He was drenched with sweat as he burst out into the deserted fifth-floor corridor and hurtled down it, following the blue and white sign to the isolation ward. He'd only run a few metres when he heard a desperate wailing coming from up ahead. It was only when he turned left into the isolation ward's observation room that he saw who was crying: a blonde woman who had her face and palms pressed against the glass window that faced onto the ward. Gabs had her arms around her, and was trying to pull her away, but the woman was screaming at her to let go. 'I won't leave my daughter. *I won't leave my daughter!*' Next to them, a brown-skinned doctor was looking very agitated, wringing his hands.

Beyond the glass, Zak could make out an occupied hospital bed, surrounded by machines. On the far side of the ward was an exterior window, through which he could see, but not hear, the chopper hovering about twenty metres beyond the building. Zak turned to the doctor. 'Help me,' he said, before sprinting across the observation room, unzipping the package that held the suit as he went. He shook it out to its full length and then, without hesitating, pulled the canvas mask he had stolen from the ambulance over his face and opened the door to the isolation ward. The doctor followed close behind while Gabs still tried to calm the little girl's now-hysterical mother.

If the little girl, lying alone on her hospital bed, had any understanding of what was happening, she didn't show it. She wore a see-through oxygen mask, and the cannula attached to her drip feed had been inserted into the back of a very limp right hand. She was awake, though, and she blinked at Zak as he approached and gently removed the oxygen mask from her face.

'What's her name?' he asked the doctor, doing his best to hide the panic from his voice.

'Ruby,' he whispered.

Zak looked over his shoulder. He could see Ruby's mother staring at him, and Gabs too.

'Do you think you can get up, Ruby? We need to put this suit on you.'

'Why?'

'I haven't got time to explain.'

'Are you a doctor?'

'You must do what he says,' the real doctor said. He pressed a button on the side of the bed that raised Ruby up into a sitting position.

It was difficult to get the suit on since Ruby was very weak. Zak and the doctor had to lift her arms up for her, and help her slip her legs into the suit. The doctor detached the cannula, then threaded it back through a flap in the suit, before zipping Ruby up.

'OK, Ruby,' Zak said. 'We need to get you out of here.'

'Why?' the little girl asked.

Zak was on the point of explaining. He didn't get the chance.

For a moment, everything happened in slow motion. There was a deafening boom and Zak heard his voice shouting 'NO!' as the whole building shook.

It felt like an earthquake had hit. Dust fell from the ceiling. The glass between the ward and the observation room shattered. So did the window, and from the corner of his eye Zak saw the chopper jerk backwards several metres from the force of the blast. The floor moved. Little Ruby fell from her bed. Zak grabbed her, and as they both tumbled to the floor, his arms automatically covered her head to protect it from any rubble that might fall her way.

The doctor fell beside them. Despite the dust, he was close enough for Zak to see what killed the man.

It was a chunk of rubble. It had fallen from the ceiling with the shaking of the building, and struck the doctor on the head as he lay on the ground. Blood flowed from his nose and his ear; the side of his face was smashed and indented. Zak reached over and felt his pulse. There was none. He had gone.

There was no time to mourn. The shock wave of the explosion had rocked Zak to his core; his visibility in the cloud of dust was less than half a metre. But somehow, now that detonation had occurred, he didn't feel scared any more. It was too late for that. The little girl was crying inside her suit. Zak had to get her out of the building. Somehow.

He could hear the thudding of the chopper's rotor blades. Other than that, and the weeping of the little girl, there was a strange kind of silence. It didn't last long. There was a deafening, sinister creaking, and Zak felt the whole building shift again.

'Zak! Are you there?' Gabs's voice, hoarse and more than a little panicked.

'Yeah . . .'

'*Ruby?*' The mother's voice was high-pitched.

'I've got her . . . the doctor's dead . . .'

Zak forced himself to his feet, lifting Ruby and her saline drip bag up at the same time. The dust stung his eyes, but through the cloud that had filled the isolation ward, he could just make out a silhouette approaching. Gabs appeared. Her blonde hair was dark grey, her face dirty. But her eyes shone with determination. 'We need to get to the roof,' she shouted.

Zak nodded, and together they picked their way through the debris of the isolation ward, Zak cradling the little girl in his arms. 'The mother's in a bad way,' Gabs shouted. 'I'll have to help her . . .'

Gabs was right. The mother's face wasn't just painted with fear, it was painted with pain. She was kneeling, surrounded by shattered glass that had cut her face in several places, holding her left arm as though it was broken. She looked stricken as Zak appeared with Ruby, but Gabs didn't give her the time to say or do anything. She helped the woman to her feet, draped her good arm around her neck and together they staggered over the uneven floor and out into the corridor.

Zak was horrified when he saw it.

The corridor itself was no longer level. The south end of it had subsided about two metres so the floor was on an incline. Huge cracks had appeared in the ceiling, and sections of the wall had collapsed. Burst pipes were spraying from both floor and ceiling, and one part of the wall had sewage dripping down it. The smell of burning reached Zak's nose. There was a fire nearby.

'That way!' Gabs pointed north just as another horrible creaking sound echoed through the whole building, and the floor beneath them shifted again. Zak looked in the direction she had pointed. There was a green emergency exit door, wonky in its frame, about fifteen metres away. Zak started towards it, struggling to carry the thin frame of little Ruby up the shifting incline. He started coughing with the dust, and sweat poured off his brow and into his already watering and stinging eyes.

Another creaking. Another shifting of the floor. 'HURRY!' Gabs shouted. 'THE BUILDING'S COLLAPSING! IT WON'T HOLD MUCH LONGER . . .'

Zak gritted his teeth and redoubled his efforts.

The emergency exit door was warped. Once he had raised the security bar, Zak tried to shoulder it open. It wouldn't budge.

'Stand back!' Gabs shouted. Zak did as he was told, to see Gabs's heel kick the door with stunning force. It flew open to reveal a set of stone stairs leading up to the roof. Zak burst through. As he ran up the cracked steps, the building gave another sickening lurch. He stumbled, and immediately heard Gabs's voice behind him. 'MOVE!'

He moved.

It was only as he emerged onto the roof of the hospital that Zak saw the full extent of the devastation the bomb had caused. The north-eastern corner of the building was already crumbling away, and the roof itself was subsiding just as the corridor had been. He was only half aware of the London skyline from up here, even though the Houses of Parliament, St Paul's Cathedral and the London Eye were all perfectly clear in the morning sun. And he only half heard the wail of sirens from the ground below. His attention was elsewhere – on the chopper that had just risen to the same height as them. Gabs had let Ruby's mother sink to the ground, and was waving her arms at the helicopter, her desperate screams of 'Over here!' lost in the chuntering noise of the rotors.

Two things happened in quick succession. The building shook, as though some giant had grabbed hold of it and was trying to rip it from its foundations. And the chopper disappeared below their line of sight.

'NO!' Zak roared. Still carrying Ruby, he sprinted to the building's edge, struggling to stay on his feet as the structure wobbled beneath him. He was five metres from the edge, however, when the chopper suddenly appeared again. It rose ten metres above the roof line, then manoeuvred itself into the centre of the building, where Gabs and Ruby's mother were waiting. One of the side doors of the chopper was open, and as Zak carried Ruby back to the others, he saw a rope being winched down, with three harnesses attached to it.

By the time he reached Gabs, she was already strapping Ruby's mum into one of the harnesses – with difficulty on account of the massive downdraught. Zak wasted no time in doing the same for the little girl in the protective suit.

Which left only one harness.

'Take it!' Zak shouted at Gabs, roaring over the noise of the chopper. But his Guardian Angel stepped away.

'Make sure they're safe, Zak,' she shouted. Her dirty face was intense, her brow furrowed. Zak knew her well enough to see that she wasn't going to discuss this. His own eyes grew flinty as he strapped himself into the remaining harness. He looked up and gave a thumbs up to the loadie in the chopper above, then put his arms around Ruby and her mother. The slack rope went taut. He felt himself being winched upwards.

And not a moment too soon.

It was almost as if the building was moaning in pain. They were barely two metres off the roof when the entire structure seemed to sink, and Gabs with it. A great crack appeared across the centre, and a huge cloud of dust ballooned up over Zak's Guardian Angel.

'Gabs!' Zak screamed. '*Gabs!*'

But there was neither sight nor sound of her.

Gabriella had disappeared.

It was as if the world had gone silent. Zak couldn't hear the thunder of the helicopter, the wailing of the little girl or the screaming of her mother. He barely saw the River Thames snaking below him, or the scenes of bedlam that were unfolding on the ground as the emergency services raced to get the hospital patients away from the collapsing building.

Time stood still.

Gabriella had disappeared!

Only as the loadie was hustling them into the body of the chopper did Zak's senses return. Two crew members were unstrapping Ruby and her mother, but Zak grabbed the loadie's arm. 'Send me back down with another harness!' he yelled. 'Quickly!'

'Forget it, son,' the loadie barked back. 'She's gone . . .'

'You don't know that,' Zak roared. And when the loadie looked uncertain, he continued to press him: 'She put her life on the line. She'd do the same for anyone. Get me back down!'

The loadie hesitated for a moment, but then he nodded. He disappeared into the body of the chopper for a moment, before returning and handing Zak a handheld beacon. 'Firefly,' he shouted as he clipped it onto Zak's harness. 'Activate it when you need to come up.'

Zak didn't even wait for the rope to slacken. He simply threw himself from the chopper's door, the two spare harnesses swirling in the downdraught around him.

The roof of the building was lost in a cloud of dust and smoke. As Zak fell forward, arms and legs splayed, he could just see flashes of orange through the cloud – the building wasn't just collapsing, it was burning. The cloud itself was hot and choking, and it seemed to cling to him and burn through his lungs as he descended into it.

His visibility was no more than half a metre. He didn't see Gabs until he was almost on top of her. She was lying on her front, choking in the smoke and trying to crawl away from a metre-wide crack that had appeared in the roof. 'Gabs!' he shouted, reaching for her, but his voice was drowned out by another terrible groan from the building. The crack in the roof creaked open, doubling in width and taking Gabs that bit further from Zak's reach. '*GABS!*' he shouted again. This time she heard him. She rolled over onto her back, an astonished expression on her terrified face.

Zak looked up. The helicopter was just a shadow above the cloud. Zak had no way of relaying to the loadie that he needed to close a gap of two metres if he was going to rescue Gabs. She scrambled uncertainly to her feet and stood on the edge of the crack in the roof.

She clearly understood that she was going to have to jump, and that Zak had to catch her.

Their eyes met. Zak held out his arms towards her. He had to force himself to stop them shaking.

What if he dropped her?

His eyes flickered to the crack in the roof. The

interior of the hospital was filled with smoke. If Gabs fell in there, she was dead. No two ways about it.

His anxiety must have shown in his face, because at that moment, Gabs gave him a reassuring grin, and winked. 'I trust you, sweetie,' she mouthed over the deafening noise all around them.

And then she jumped.

It was as if her jump was a signal. There was an enormous rumbling from the heart of the building as the structure finally gave way entirely. Zak felt Gabs's right hand grab his wrist, and he locked his own hand around hers. He felt the extra weight strain against the rope. As Gabs dangled over the collapsing building, he used his left hand to activate the firefly. It flashed brightly in the dust cloud, which had suddenly grown twice as thick. Instantly they started to ascend.

As they emerged from the smoke, Zak concentrated on keeping hold of his mentor. But as the helicopter carried them away from the blast site and over the sparkling blue waters of the Thames, he couldn't help but stare at the remnants of the hospital. Thirty minutes ago it had been a gleaming, shining block of glass and mirrors, as solid as any other building around it. Now it was a mass of rubble surrounded by billowing plumes of smoke.

The latest scene of devastation wreaked by a bomber whose motives were as unknown as his, or her, identity.

A bomber who they were no closer to locating, and who doubtless had more pyrotechnics up his or her sleeve.

11

DISHONOURABLE DISCHARGE

In a small flat on the top floor of a tower block somewhere in West London, a man watched the breaking television news.

Apart from the wooden chair he was sitting in, there was no furniture in this flat. Just boxes. Boxes and boxes and boxes, collected and stored here over the years. In these boxes, there was enough explosive to bring down not only this tower block, but the three others nearby. He wouldn't be destroying blocks of flats with his arsenal, however. He was chasing bigger game than that.

There was no hint of emotion on his face as he watched the live TV reports from the south bank of the Thames. But that didn't mean he felt none. Quite the contrary. He felt angry. More angry than he had done for years, his anger fuelled from a simmering resentment since he had found that he finally had a chance to do what he had wished to do for so long. But the destruction of the building was not enough. He needed *lives* for maximum impact. That was why he had watched the news of his little present at Pimlico tube station with something like satisfaction. He didn't mourn the dead. They would be forgotten soon enough. They always were. It was his campaign of terror that would linger in people's memories.

It seemed astonishing to him that anybody other than the one person already in on his game could have noticed his code. But having staked out the house of the Puzzle Master – what a ridiculous name – he realized they had. And watching the television now, one thing was obvious: the device in the hospital had been discovered.

He glanced down at his lap. A tablet computer showed a map of the South Bank area. A small red dot flashed just where the hospital used to be. It meant the vehicle he was tracking – the one onto which he had slipped the tracking device – was on site.

Did that mean his code, so carefully constructed, had been cracked? He had to assume that it did. He had planned for London to have one day to breathe, one more day to live in fear in terror. That way, the impact of his third device would be all the greater. And he knew that the third crossword was primed and ready to send to the newspaper from his laptop computer. Giving him this crossword had, in fact, been one of the last acts of the Puzzle Master's life and he smiled as he recalled the man's horror as he had produced the rope that would be the ending of it. But now he couldn't risk sending it in. He would have to use his backup plan to get his message out. A shame, but there was nothing for it.

There was something else he had to do too. Something important. He had seen the three figures entering the Puzzle Master's house that morning, and he knew they were the flies in his ointment.

There was only one thing you could do to flies, he thought to himself as he stood up and turned off the television set.

Swat them.

The chopper set Zak and Gabs with Ruby and her mother down on the helipad at the top of an office block half a mile down river. Once Gabs and Zak had their feet on the ground, the flight crew – who clearly didn't quite know what to make of this strange duo that had just risked their lives in such a spectacular way – wanted to transport them to RAF Northolt. Gabs flatly refused to get back on the helicopter. She made one call on her mobile. Minutes later, the flight crew received instruction to take Ruby and her mother to another hospital, and to leave their other passengers where they were. They left Gabs and Zak and flew away.

It felt strange emerging, filthy and sweat-soaked, onto street level as though nothing had happened to them. Even though they looked a mess, nobody gave them a second glance. Word of the bomb was on all the news channels, and the dust cloud was clearly visible in the June skies. The roads were solid with traffic, the windscreens of the cars grimy with the smoke that had spread through the air. Pedestrians were either talking excitedly in little groups, coughing or walking fast with their heads down. Zak noticed several shopkeepers pulling closed the security grilles in front of their shop windows, clearly deciding not to open in the wake of what had happened.

They stood for a moment, watching the chaotic scenes in the street. And then Gabs took Zak by the shoulders and hugged him. 'Thank you, sweetie,' she whispered.

'You'd have done the same for me,' he replied, slightly embarrassed by her sudden show of affection. And it was true. She would have done.

Back to the Knightsbridge flat, where Michael

and Raf met them, and listened silently as Gabs explained what had happened. They cleaned themselves up – Zak found scrapes and bruises all over his body that he didn't know he had, but was otherwise mercifully unharmed – and then he tried to grab some sleep.

He managed only a couple of hours' shut-eye. It was haunted by images of hanged men and buzzing flies; of shadowy faces with snubnose rounds whizzing past, and sometimes into, their heads; of little girls in white protective suits and buildings collapsing into mushroom clouds of smoke. He woke up feeling worse, not better.

And then his surreal day got even stranger.

Sitting in the main room with Michael, Raf and Gabs on the sofa opposite him, Zak found one corner of his mind wondering if Michael had slept at all. Wondering if he *ever* slept.

Then wondering what on *earth* he was talking about.

'Congratulations, Zak,' Michael began. 'So far as we can tell, there were no casualties. I think it's reasonable for you to take the credit for that.'

'There was one casualty,' Zak replied quietly, remembering the doctor. 'The doctor with the little girl, up on the top floor. He wouldn't leave his patient. I saw him die. It wasn't nice.'

'A brave man,' Michael replied. 'And I'll make sure his actions are noted, that his family are informed of the circumstances of his death.' He paused and there was a moment of respectful silence before he continued, 'But we won't achieve anything by mourning him. So I've landed you an office job.'

Zak blinked. 'Job?' he asked weakly.

'Well, I *say* "job". They won't be *paying* you, of course. Think of it as work experience. I'm told there's a very long list of people waiting for a similar position, but we've managed to queue barge—'

Zak held up one hand. 'Hang on,' he interrupted. He took a moment to gather his thoughts. 'Work experience *where*?'

Michael looked slightly surprised at the question. 'The *Daily Post*, of course. Something's clearly going on there, and we need to find out what. Nobody's going to notice the new work experience boy, so long as you just keep your head down and your ears open.'

Zak closed his eyes and squeezed the bridge of his nose, trying to keep his mind straight. 'I still don't understand,' he said. 'Just because the Puzzle Master worked for the *Post*, and that's where the puzzles appeared, it doesn't mean that somebody at the newspaper is involved in all this.'

'True,' Michael conceded. 'Not on its own. But

we examined Mr Hinton's phone records. The *Post*'s switchboard routed calls to his number at the times stated in those notes he left. And don't forget, he did give us a lead to follow.'

Zak thought back to what he had read in the dead man's notebook. *I wish I knew who he was. Someone at the newspaper, I suspect. Ludgrove? I've met him a few times. He's a rotten apple . . .*

'Ludgrove?' he asked.

'Precisely. Gabs, you have something on this Ludgrove, I believe?'

Gabs nodded, then started to read from a file. She did not have the demeanour of someone who had just narrowly escaped death. 'Joshua Ludgrove,' she said in a clear voice. 'Defence correspondent. Lives at number six Galsheils Avenue, Tottenham. Formerly a private in the British Army. Dishonourable discharge, though he'd rather keep that quiet.'

'Do we know why the army booted him out?' Raf asked quietly.

'Cowardice,' Gabs stated. 'His unit was posted to Northern Ireland in the early 1970s. Ludgrove refused to go. His journalism is very critical of the British government and its defence policies, and by all accounts he's a rather nasty piece of work.'

'Ludgrove is on MI5's watch list,' Michael continued. 'There have been suggestions in the past that he has been on the payroll of a number of foreign intelligence services, but nobody's ever been able to make it stick. Keep a close eye on him, Zak. I don't want Private Ludgrove to so much as sneeze without you knowing it, OK?'

Zak nodded. He looked at Gabs and then Raf. 'What about you two?' he asked. 'What are you going to do?'

Michael answered before they could speak. 'Gabriella and Raphael have other work to do,' he said. 'Don't underestimate this Ludgrove character, Zak. Cowards make the worst kind of bullies, and if he's mixed up in all this, he's an extremely dangerous man.' He stood up and gazed out of the window that looked over the London skyline. There was still a faint pall of smoke on the south side of the river, the memory of that morning's explosion. 'You're not in Mexico or Africa now,' he continued. 'This is a different sort of operation. Just familiar old London. But don't let that lull you into a false sense of security. Our bomber has no scruples. He'll kill innocent men and women on the underground, and sick children in a hospital. That means familiar old London is one of the riskiest places in the world right now. It's our job to make it safe again.'

He turned and looked back at them. 'From now

on, all three of you check in with me every two hours by holding down number one on the keypads of your phones for five seconds. Check-in times are between five to and five past the hour. If you miss one for any reason, wait until the next check-in time. Do not check in outside these times. If I receive an unexpected check-in, I'll know something untoward has happened and that somebody is impersonating or coercing you. Understood?'

'Understood,' the three of them replied.

'We regroup here every evening at 1900 hours. And I want information, Zak. Evidence. I want to be absolutely certain Ludgrove's our man before we bring him in. OK?'

Zak nodded. 'OK,' he said.

'Good.' Michael pressed the tips of his fingers together and surveyed Zak from over them. 'Tell me, Zak,' he said, and suddenly, after the solemn seriousness of the conversation, the old twinkle had returned to his green eyes. 'Have you ever taken a keen interest in ornithology?'

'In what?'

'Ornithology. Bird-watching. Have you ever experienced the pleasures of lying for hours in long, wet grass waiting for the lesser-spotted something-or-other to rise?'

'Er, can't say I have.'

'Shame.' Michael continued to stare at him from above his fingertips.

'Have *you*?' Zak ventured.

'Not since my days in the Scouts,' the man answered. 'Never had the time, somehow.'

'Right. So, er, why do you ask?'

'Did I mention the work experience?' Michael asked, sounding innocent.

'Yeah . . .' Zak replied slowly. 'With Ludgrove, right?'

'Wrong. It would look a little obvious if we shoe-horned you into working alongside him, wouldn't you say. Happily, however, the *Daily Post* is one of the few newspapers left who print a daily nature notes column. You'll be working on that. And you'll need to come across as a keen bird-watcher – a twitcher – so here's a bit of reading for you.' He tossed Zak a small battered guide to British birds.

Was Zak imagining it, or was Michael – serious, stern Michael – biting the inside of his cheeks in an attempt not to laugh? Gabs showed no such restraint. She was openly grinning. 'You know, Raf?' she said, 'I've always thought there was something of the Bill Oddie about our Zak.'

'It's the hair,' Raf said gravely. 'Scruffy.'

'Er, excuse me,' Zak said, unable to keep the note of outrage from his voice. 'I don't know if any of you remember, but I've had quite a busy couple of days. Why am I the one that has to go and sit around some boring newspaper office talking about the lesser-spotted . . . whatever it is?'

Michael suddenly grew serious again. 'I've already told you, Zak. Nobody notices the work-experience boy. And don't for a minute think that this isn't important work. Lives could depend on how well you do it.'

Chastened, Zak fell silent. He watched as Michael pulled a cigarette case from his inside pocket and lit the pungent cherry tobacco he favoured. The smell instantly filled the whole room.

'The Puzzle Master's anonymous tormentor wanted him to plant three crosswords in the paper,' Michael continued. 'I think we can reasonably assume that this points to three separate bombings. You have very cleverly identified two of them and our analysts have now examined the crossword the *Daily Post* are planning to run tomorrow. It gives no indication of a third device. Of course, it may be that the third message is encrypted differently to the first two, but I'd say that was rather unlikely. I suspect either that the perpetrator saw the evacuation of the hospital and is holding off for a few days, or that he's giving London a breather before his final spectacular. I don't know about you, though, but I'd rather not sit around waiting for it. Agreed?'

'Agreed,' said Zak.

'Excellent. I suggest you catch up on some reading – not only the bird book, but also Ludgrove's file.' He nodded at Gabs, who passed Zak a brown file with the name LUDGROVE pencilled on the front, then Michael continued. 'Get some sleep too. Master Harry Gold is expected at the offices of the *Daily Post* at eight o'clock tomorrow morning.' He stood up. 'Gabriella, Raphael, you'll need to come with me.' He headed towards the door, but had only gone a couple of metres before he stopped and turned, slapping the palm of his hand dramatically against his forehead. 'I almost forgot,' he said. He reached into his pocket and pulled out a photograph, which he handed to Zak. It showed a middle-aged man, rather paunchy, with unfashionable circular glasses that were wonky on his face, and an unkempt, greying beard.

'Who's this?' Zak asked.

The mischievous sparkle had returned to Michael's eyes. 'Your new boss,' he said. 'The *Daily Post*'s nature correspondent. You'll need to ask for him when you get there in the morning.'

'What's his name?'

'Rodney,' said Michael.

'Rodney?'

'That's right, Zak. Rodney. Rodney Hendricks. I'm sure you'll get on like a house on fire. Word is he's fond of a pint or two at lunch time. That should give you ample time for snooping.'

Gabs sighed. 'I do wish he'd stop using that word,' she said to nobody in particular.

'Why? It's what we do, isn't it?'

'Of course. But it sounds so uncouth.'

Michael shrugged. 'Not as uncouth as killing hundreds of innocent people,' he said. And without another word, he led Gabs and Raf out of the flat, leaving Zak alone with the picture of his new boss, the file on Joshua Ludgrove, and his thoughts.

Gabs had been right. Everything in Ludgrove's file suggested he was a nasty piece of work. Zak was surprised at how detailed it was. He'd been expelled from two schools for bullying and had joined the army at the age of sixteen because his father, himself a military man, had insisted on it. The bullying hadn't stopped when he joined the armed forces. The file contained seven notes from his commanding officer stating that he had received complaints of both physical and verbal violence from the young Ludgrove. There were two complaints that he had stolen personal property from his fellow recruits. On being discharged from the army, he had found himself a job on a local newspaper, lying about his CV in the process. From there, he had worked his way up the ladder. He had been married once. It had lasted six months before she left, complaining that he beat her up, although she never pressed charges. Reading between the lines, Zak deduced that it was his ability to bully a story out of people that made him such a good journalist.

He put the file to one side, stretched out on the sofa and switched on the TV – he needed a pause before trying to become a sudden fount of knowledge on the habits of sparrows. The same reporter he had watched at St Peter's Crag was talking breathlessly, but it was the constantly updated ribbon of text along the bottom of the screen that grabbed Zak's attention. 1 ADULT CONFIRMED MISSING PRESUMED DEAD IN HOSPITAL BOMBING . . . PRIME MINISTER: 'IT IS A MIRACLE NO MORE PEOPLE WERE HURT IN THIS COWARDLY ACT. MY THANKS GO TO THE EMERGENCY AND SECURITY SERVICES FOR THEIR OUTSTANDING WORK.' . . . 37 CONFIRMED DEAD IN TUBE BOMBING. 60 STILL MISSING. RESCUE WORKERS SAY CHANCES OF FINDING ANY FURTHER SURVIVORS ARE 'SMALL' . . . MIDNIGHT GUNSHOTS REPORTED IN VICINITY OF HARRINGTON SECURE HOSPITAL, SOUTH LONDON. METROPOLITAN POLICE

HAVE ISSUED REQUEST FOR MEMBERS OF THE PUBLIC WHO SAW ANYTHING SUSPICIOUS TO COME FORWARD ... CHIEF COMMISSIONER AND HOME SECRETARY CONFIRM TERRORISM THREAT LEVEL HAS INCREASED TO 'CRITICAL' FOR THE FIRST TIME SINCE 7/7. LON-DONERS URGED TO BE 'EXTREMELY VIGILANT', AND REASSURED THAT THE SECURITY SERVICES ARE TAKING 'ALL POSSIBLE PRECAUTIONS AT THIS TIME OF HIGH ALERT'.

Zak stared at those words. All possible pre-cautions at this time of high alert? If only that were true. Michael was right. Three crosswords surely meant three bombings, and at the moment they were barely any closer to working out where or when the third bombing was going to take place.

And time, as it had a habit of doing, was running out.

17 JUNE

12

NY HERO

London had changed.

The Victoria Line was still down, of course, on account of the Pimlico bombing just two days ago. Every other line was delayed. The passengers on buses and even pedestrians on the street eyed each other with suspicion and Zak noticed glimpses of fear on the faces of many going down the steps to the tube.

He was standing on the edge of Victoria railway station, near those stairs, holding a free newspaper someone had just shoved into his fist. On the front cover was the hospital at the moment of collapse, and the picture quite clearly showed the chopper with two people dangling from it on a rope. The journalists had enlarged the image of Zak and Gabs, but their faces were blurred and unrecognizable, thank God. It would be difficult for him to keep a low profile if everyone at the newspaper – many of them digging into the news story around the bombs – had seen his features. He heard two sirens in the distance, both travelling in different directions. When one of them faded away, a third came into earshot. The area itself was swarming with flak-jacketed armed police.

Yes. London had changed. It was a city on the edge of panic, and it had good reason to be.

Zak had changed too, in the months that had passed since he last considered himself a Londoner. Changed since he had lived with Ellie and her parents in Camden, gone to school like any normal teenager, hung round the park at the weekends. Now he immediately picked out the MP5s clipped to the jackets of the armed police teams and his mind automatically processed everything he knew about that weapon. Nine mill rounds, rate of fire 800 rounds per minute. But it wasn't that he could identify a firearm with the same ease as other kids his own age could identify a new model of mobile phone that made him realize how different he was. It was that he was looking at the world in a different way. By the entrance to M&S, ten metres to his eleven o'clock, he saw a man in a leather jacket surreptitiously raise his sleeve to his mouth, and his lips move. The armed police, he realized, were just a visible sign of security. There were covert personnel in situ too, whom ordinary members of the public would never notice.

'No loitering, son.' One of the armed officers had approached him. Zak nodded and hitched his rucksack over his shoulder. He made to leave, but the officer held up one palm. 'Hold your horses,' he said.

'Something wrong?' Zak asked, innocently.

'Open your rucksack, please.' His words were polite, but his tone of voice wasn't.

Zak did as he was asked. The officer poked around inside, but found nothing more exciting than a couple of rounds of cheese sandwiches, the battered guide to birds and a Harry Potter book that was well thumbed even though Zak hadn't read a word of it. The officer nodded. 'On your way,' he said, before turning his attention to a confused-looking Japanese tourist. Zak left the area.

The offices of the *Daily Post* were situated on the top two floors of an office building 100 metres to the north of Victoria Station. Zak walked through the revolving glass door into the building's comfortable reception area at eight a.m. precisely. He removed his phone from his pocket and held down number one on the keypad, checking in with

Michael almost absent-mindedly as the rest of his attention focused on the layout of his surroundings. Second exit, fifteen metres to his left. A barrier to the right of the reception desk, blocking the reception from the area around the lifts. As he approached the desk, a receptionist looked over her half-moon glasses at a sheet of paper.

'Yes?' she asked impatiently.

'My name's Harry Gold. I'm here to see Rodney Hendricks.'

Thirty seconds passed as she tapped at a keyboard and peered at her computer screen.

'Harry Gold, did you say?'

'That's right,' Zak replied, quietly and politely. 'G – O – L—'

'No Harry Gold here, young man,' she said. 'Are you sure you have the right place? This is a newspaper office, you know. Who are you supposed to be visiting again?'

'Rodney Hendricks.'

'I say, did I hear my name?'

Zak looked around. Standing behind him was the man whose photo he had seen. He was about his own height but a good deal older – comfortably in his fifties. His little round glasses made him look rather like a mole and his blue eyes sparkled, making his ruddy face look very jolly. Zak was bizarrely put in mind of Father Christmas. If Rodney Hendricks had been wearing a red outfit instead of his crumpled grey suit, the similarity would have been astonishing.

'Hi, Mr Hendricks,' Zak said offering his hand. 'I'm Harry. Harry . . .'

'Harry Gold? Yes, of course, of course. I must say, it's jolly nice of head office to send me a bit of help. Usually it's the news desk who get all the work experience. Or features, of course. Mustn't forget features. Don't worry, Elspeth, I'll take him up. Follow me, Harry, follow me.'

The words tumbled out of Hendricks's mouth as though he couldn't stop them. They continued to tumble as Hendricks led him across the marble reception towards the lift.

'So, young Harry, what brings you to the hallowed halls of the fourth estate? Hundred years old, the *Daily Post*, m'boy. Rich in tradition. British institution. Floors seven and eight, m'boy, we'll be needing seven.' He pressed the button to call the lift, then stuck his hands in his pocket and stood there, whistling rather aimlessly as the lift rose from the basement level.

'I'm hoping to be a journalist,' Zak said, repeating the story he had worked out yesterday. 'I have an uncle who—'

'Eh?'

'I was just saying that—'

'Ah, here we are!' The lift doors slid open. 'After you, m'boy. After . . . Ah, Ludgrove . . . what an unexpected pleasure.' Hendricks didn't sound like it was a pleasure at all. He looked at the solitary figure in the lift. He was tall – much taller than Zak or Hendricks – and thick-set. He was very cleanly shaven, with the exception of a mole on his left cheek from which three hairs sprung. His hair was very precisely combed into a centre parting, and his forehead was creased into what looked like a permanent frown. In his right hand he held a ball-point pen. Every couple of seconds, his thumb pressed the button at the end of the pen a couple of times, clicking the nib in and out.

'Hendricks,' Ludgrove said without much enthusiasm.

Click click. Click click.

'In you go, Harry m'boy. After you, chop chop.'

There was something about Ludgrove. Zak sensed it the moment he stepped into the lift. It was like he had an invisible force field of contempt around him. 'Yeah,' the *Daily Post*'s defence correspondent said. 'It would be a great shame for the nature notes desk to go unmanned. How would the newspaper possibly survive?'

'Very popular, the nature notes, Harry m'boy,' Hendricks said, ignoring the barely concealed criticism. 'Very, very popular.'

'Right up there with the horoscopes,' Ludgrove said with a sneer. 'Or the TV listings.'

Click click. Click click.

'Or the crossword?' Zak asked.

He was watching Ludgrove carefully when he said it. He noticed the tightening of his eyes, and the irritable glance he flashed Zak. And he noticed the way the clicking stopped. But there was no time for Ludgrove to reply. A gentle chime announced their arrival on the seventh floor. The doors hissed open and Ludgrove barged his way out, clicking the ballpoint once again as he went. Hendricks scratched his beard. He had a slightly confused look on his face, like a school child who had just been bullied and didn't know what to say about it. 'Funny old cove, Ludgrove,' he said. 'Best to stay clear of him, eh?'

The lift doors started to shut. Zak stopped them with his foot and they slid open again. 'Should we—'

'Yes!' Hendricks said, as though he had suddenly woken up. 'Onwards!' He shuffled out of the lift and onto the seventh floor.

The vast open-plan office of the *Daily Post* was

very busy. As Hendricks led Zak through a maze of glass desks, computer terminals and whirring photocopiers, he estimated that there must be at least a hundred people working here, but they were doing just that: working, not talking. There was a constant *clackety-clack* of computer keyboards as journalists typed up stories. Anybody on the phone spoke in a loud voice just to be heard above the hubbub. As Hendricks and Zak passed through the office, the nature notes correspondent greeted his colleagues in a breezy voice. 'Alan . . . Pippa . . . morning, George, morning, Emma.' The Alans, Pippas, Georges and Emmas didn't reply, but Zak felt their eyes on him as he passed. They clearly all thought Rodney Hendricks was a bit of a weirdo and, as he was with him, the opinion extended to Zak too.

Hendricks's desk was in a far corner of the office, just next to the toilets. It was covered in books and papers, and had a very old computer. Hendricks stared at the chaos, then started rather ineffectively to move some of the papers around. 'You'll be needing somewhere to sit,' he murmured, slightly flustered.

Zak couldn't help smiling. 'Why don't I find us both a cup of tea?' he suggested.

'Of course, m'boy,' Hendricks said without looking at him. 'Kettle that way.' He waved vaguely at the centre of the room. Zak went exploring.

Now that he was no longer with Hendricks, Zak could immediately see that Michael had been right. Nobody noticed him. He found he could wander among the desks with barely a glance from the journalists sitting at them. As he walked, he caught glimpses of half-formed headlines. SECOND BOMBING . . . POLICE BAFFLED . . . MINISTER CALLS FOR CALM . . . There was no doubt that this would be the big story for several days to come.

What Hendricks had referred to as a kettle was in fact an urn of boiling water surrounded by a collection of plastic cups, teabags and instant coffee granules. Three moveable screens surrounded the table on which they sat to form a makeshift room in the centre of the open-plan office, but at the corners where the screens met there was a gap of a couple of inches. Zak peered nonchalantly through these gaps as he made two cups of tea. About ten metres beyond one of them, he could see a large window with an impressive vista over London. Through it, he could just see the roof of Buckingham Palace, a Union Jack on the flagpole hanging limply. He remembered going to see the Changing of the Guard when he was much younger. His mum had told him that if the flag was up, it meant the Queen was at home. Zak was older now, and a bit wiser. He wondered if she was really there, given that the city was on high terror alert.

It took a few moments for Zak to realize what else he could see. Between the window and the gap where the screens met, about five metres away, was a glass desk, much neater than Hendricks's. Its occupant sat with his back to Zak. His right elbow was resting on the arm of his chair and he was holding a ballpoint in his fist.

Click click. Click click. Ludgrove.

Between Ludgrove's body and his forearm, Zak could just make out a small section of the computer screen. He could see a line of text, cut off at the beginning and the end. It read: '. . . NY HER . . .'

Click click. Click click.

Zak edged forward, leaning over the table holding the hot-water urn. He squinted, hoping that Ludgrove would move his arm enough for Zak to see more of what was written on his screen. Was the next letter an 'O'? Or maybe a 'D' . . . ?

Suddenly, Ludgrove spun round. It was almost as if he had sensed Zak's eyes on him. His gaze pierced the gap between the screening panels and his dark eyes narrowed. As quickly as he had spun round to catch Zak staring at him, he twirled his seat again and clicked his mouse. His computer screen went blank.

'Ah, Harry, m'boy.' Now it was Zak's turn to spin round. Hendricks was there, peering at him from behind his little round glasses, a leather-bound book in his hands. 'Come along, come along, I've something most fascinating for you . . .' He shuffled out of the tea-making area and back to his desk. Zak followed him, but as he glanced over his shoulder, he saw Ludgrove staring at him with thinly veiled suspicion. Zak cursed his lack of subtlety. Things hadn't started well.

Hendricks's desk was only slightly tidier. The bearded man had swiped a spot for Zak on the opposite side and found a chair from somewhere which he'd placed in front of this gap in the mess. Zak accepted a sheaf of papers from him. 'The sparrow!' Hendricks said, as though he were announcing an Oscar winner.

Zak looked down at the paper uncomprehendingly. 'Er . . . what about it?' he asked.

'On the move, m'boy. Leaving this sceptred isle, escaping to pastures new. Or at least, we think it is. I've asked readers of my column to count the number of sparrows they've seen over the past week.' A troubled look crossed his face. He rummaged around his desk a little more, lifted up a pile of paper and with a triumphant 'Ha!' pulled another sheaf of papers, at least as large as the first, from underneath and handed it to Zak. 'Fabulous response,' Hendricks said. 'Bit of bore for an old brain like mine to deal with. Wonder if you might log 'em all.' He patted his elderly computer screen, then turned it round so that it was facing Zak. 'Not my thing, really, Harry m'boy, but it's got to be easier for you than for me. And besides, I have an article to pen on the fascinating subject of the long-tailed shrike.'

'The what?'

'The long-tailed shrike, my dear boy. Don't tell me you haven't heard of it.'

'Er, 'fraid not.'

'Ah, well it *is* rather rare. A vagrant in fact, only landing in the British Isles by accident. But quite lovely. Quite, *quite* lovely . . .'

Hendricks continued to state just *how* lovely while Zak looked rather gloomily down at the pieces of paper in his hand. There had to be at least 500. He glanced towards Ludgrove's desk – he was no longer there. If Zak refused Hendricks's request, or even moaned about it, he could be out of here a minute later. That would have been fine by him, but Michael might have a thing or two to say about it. He sighed, and took a seat at the desk. If he made a start on this boring job now, he could have a snoop around the offices while Hendricks wasn't there.

'Look lively, m'boy,' Hendricks said in a low voice. 'Editor's on his way.'

The editor was a short man with a pot belly and hair that sprouted from the top of his open-necked shirt. He had a rather harassed look on his face, and clearly didn't even notice Zak's presence. 'Hendricks!' he barked. 'I want a piece for tomorrow's paper on the environmental effect of this blasted explosion on the wildlife of the city. Got it?'

'I beg your pardon?' Hendricks said, his voice quietly shocked.

'I said, I want a—'

'That will be quite impossible.'

The editor blinked at him. '*What?*'

'It will by *quite* impossible. I'm preparing an article on the long-tailed shrike.'

The editor looked at him as if he was mad. All of a sudden, Hendricks started to read from the pad on his desk, holding one arm in front of him like an actor. '*Quiet, graceful, powerful!*' he announced. '*Every person near Yarmouth will witness jaw-dropping, Xanadu-like tails, unbelievably splendid swooping and diving as flocks of this rare bird, seldom seen in the British Isles, flock to the south coast . . .*'

The editor's face went a little red. 'Hendricks, you can stuff your long-tailed whatever-it-is. I don't want a single piece in tomorrow's paper that isn't about bombs. Do I make myself clear?'

Hendricks looked shocked. 'But—'

The editor didn't let him finish. He grabbed the piece of paper Hendricks had been writing on, crumpled it up and threw it to the floor like a child having a tantrum. '*Do I make myself clear?*'

Their gazes locked. 'Quite clear,' Hendricks murmured, suddenly contrite. 'Of course.'

'*Thank* you.' The editor stomped away and started shouting at somebody else on the other side of the newsroom while Hendricks picked up the crumpled piece of paper from the floor.

For a few minutes, Hendricks mumbled into his beard, but he soon recovered his good temper. To Zak's chagrin, he showed no signs of leaving his desk. He sat there for the next hour, wittering away almost nonstop as he browsed through the paper on his desk and buried his nose into the various wildlife books that were scattered around. 'The grebe, Harry, marvellous bird, wonder if our readers might like a little piece on the grebe one of these days . . . Ah, the starling! Underrated. I could write a book on the starling, Harry m'boy, but twitchers are a funny lot. They have their favourites like everyone, I suppose . . .'

Soon Hendricks's voice just became part of the

background. An hour passed, as Zak entered the mind-numbingly boring data on the sheets in front of him: names, addresses, number of sparrows spotted.

Ten a.m. Check-in. Twelve a.m. Check-in again. By now, Zak had developed the skill of nodding at the right moment to make it appear that he was listening. In fact, as he typed, the cogs in his mind were turning . . . *NY HER* . . . Ludgrove could have been reading anything, of course, but he'd seemed extremely keen to switch off his screen when he'd seen Zak watching. What had it said? NY – did that stand for New York? HER – if the next letter was an O, it spelled HERO. New York Hero. What could that mean?

He was never going to find anything out stuck here at a desk in a corner of the office. He needed an excuse to get away from Hendricks. Making a cup of tea or nipping to the loo wasn't good enough. He wanted to find out what had been on Ludgrove's screen.

The answer, he realized, was staring him in the face.

He was inputting his data into an Excel spreadsheet. Hendricks couldn't see the screen. Even if he could, Zak reckoned he would be so absorbed talking about the native ladybird that he wouldn't notice what Zak was about to do. He minimized the screen, navigated to the system files of the hard drive, copied one of them to another location and then deleted the original. When he tried to relaunch Excel, an error message appeared on the screen.

'And you see, Harry, m'boy, the trouble with these invasive species is that they have a terrible effect on the—'

'Um, Mr Hendricks?'

'Call me Rodney, m'boy.'

'There's something wrong with my computer.'

A slightly panicked look crossed Hendricks's face. He stood up, walked round to Zak's side of the table and scratched his beard as he looked at the error message, clearly baffled. 'Oh dear,' he said. 'We'll have to call the IT boys in.'

'Don't worry,' Zak said quickly. 'I'll go and find them. I could do with stretching my legs.'

Hendricks looked momentarily uncertain, but then he smiled. 'Of course, m'boy. But hurry back, eh? Important work. You'll find them down in the basement. Gloomy old place. Don't care for it myself . . .' He shuffled back round to his side of the desk where he picked up his book again. Zak crossed the office floor. When he was halfway to the lift he looked back. Hendricks was totally immersed, but a quick look in the other direction told him that

Ludgrove was watching him leave.

There was something about his gaze that made the skin on the back of Zak's neck tingle. He suppressed the desire to return the defence correspondent's stare. He'd already done enough to arouse suspicion and he knew he had to be more careful. He also knew he had to examine the contents of Ludgrove's computer. It was like an itch that needed scratching. Trying to sit at the screen was too clumsy and obvious. There were a hundred others in this room who would notice him sitting where he shouldn't be. Which meant finding a back way. Hacking into the newspaper's intranet. Once he had done that, he could have all the access he wanted.

Zak Darke stood in front of the closed lift doors and pressed the button marked 'B'.

13

LIQUID LUNCH

Four people stood silently in the lift as he descended – three men, one woman. None of them spoke, to Zak or to each other, and they all stepped out on the ground floor, leaving Zak to get to the basement alone.

The doors slid open onto a deserted corridor. To his right, a mop leaning against the bare wall and, ten metres beyond that, a green door marked FIRE EXIT. Someone had taped a piece of paper onto the wall opposite him. The letters 'IT' were scrawled on it, and an arrow to the left. Zak followed the corridor along and to the right. He reached an open door that led into a large, windowless room. There was one man in here in his early twenties. He appeared to be playing *Call of Duty* on one of the eight large terminals dotted around the room. A heavy, metallic drilling sound of gunfire came from his machine, and because it was gloomy down here in the basement, his face glowed with the light of the screen.

Zak coughed to announce his presence. The guy looked up from his game.

'Yeah?'

Zak stepped into the room. 'I've got a problem with my computer,' he said.

'Tried turning it off and on again?' the guy said in a bored voice, all his attention back on his computer game.

'Yes,' Zak replied. 'I tried that. No luck.'

The *Call of Duty* boy sighed – he obviously considered Zak to be an unwelcome interruption to his gaming session – pressed a button on his screen to pause the game and stood up. With obvious reluctance, he stomped over to another terminal.

Zak stepped further into the room. 'I didn't get your name,' he said.

'Darren.' The IT guy was sitting at a second terminal directly opposite the one on which he was playing his game. 'What computer you using?' he asked.

'Rodney Hendricks's.'

Darren's eyes rolled as if to say, not him again. 'Quite sure he switched it on in the first place, are you?'

Zak forced a smile at the IT man's little joke, then indicated the chair he'd just vacated. 'Mind if I sit down.'

'S'long as you don't touch anything. Getting a high score on that thing. Got a high score last week and all . . .'

Zak sat down in front of the *Call of Duty* screen. It showed an assault rifle aimed in the direction of three Taliban fighters, their heads wrapped in keffiyahs, and a snow-topped mountain range in the background. As Darren's fingers flew over the keyboard of his new terminal, however, Zak nonchalantly pressed the ESC key and the game screen shrank to a normal-sized window, which he quickly minimized.

'I've got remote access,' Darren announced. 'What's wrong then?'

'Excel,' Zak said. 'Not loading.' He clicked the remote access icon on his own screen. A window popped up with a list of names. He scanned down until he found 'Ludgrove, J'. He double-clicked on the name. A password-entry box appeared.

'Hey!'

Zak started. He looked up at Darren.

'You been messing with the system files?'

Zak glanced guiltily at the *Call of Duty* computer, before realizing Darren was talking about the one upstairs. 'I haven't touched them,' he said.

'Well someone has,' Darren grunted. 'In the last ten minutes too. Moved a .exe file from the system folder. Anyone else been at your machine?'

'No. Actually . . . yes.'

'Who?'

'Another work-experience guy. Black hair. Wears a green tie. Don't know his name.' As Zak spun his lie, Darren stood up and started walking back to his original terminal. Zak felt his pulse racing as he clicked cancel then maximized the *Call of Duty* screen again. 'I'll have a word with him, shall I? Tell him to . . .' Darren was right next to him now, looking meaningfully at the seat Zak had taken. 'Sorry . . .' Zak jumped up. 'Anyway, thanks.'

Darren grunted again. The sounds of his game filled the room almost before he was sitting down.

Zak was halfway to the door when he suddenly turned, as though something had just struck him. 'You know what?' he said.

'What?'

'That work-experience dude. I think I saw him on someone else's computer. Better make sure he didn't mess that one up too.'

Darren dragged his eyes away from the screen to give Zak a sour look. He paused his game for a second time, then started walking back over to the other computer.

Zak moved quickly but stealthily. Pulling his phone from his pocket, he swiped the screen and tapped the camera icon, all the while moving in the direction of the second terminal. As Darren sat down, Zak took up position directly behind him, aiming the camera lens at the IT man's fingers, and in full view of the screen.

'Whose computer was he messing with, then?' Darren asked.

'I think his name's "Lud" something . . . Ludlow?'

'Ludgrove,' Darren said. He brought up the remote access screen and double-clicked on Ludgrove's name. His fingers touch-typed a password. Zak couldn't make it out, but he was confident that his camera had recorded the IT man's fingers on the keyboard. He switched off the phone and turned his attention to the screen.

Darren was scrolling backwards through a list of all the actions performed on Ludgrove's computer, each line coded with the time the action was performed. A Google search at 11.38. An email sent eleven minutes before that. Darren continued to scroll, and as nothing out of the ordinary presented itself, he didn't stop until he reached 8.27. Just minutes, Zak worked out, after he had seen Ludgrove's screen.

08.27 File deleted
File deleted
File deleted
File deleted

08.26 File deleted
File deleted
File deleted

Darren didn't seem to find anything unusual. 'Looks kosher,' he said. 'Still, I'd better tell Ludgrove if you think someone was fiddlin' . . .'

'Don't worry,' Zak said quickly and with a friendly smile. 'I'm going back up there now. I'll tell him.'

The IT man looked uncertain for a moment. Then his eyes flickered towards his *Call of Duty* terminal. 'Sweet,' he muttered lazily, and he slouched back to his game.

By the time Zak left the room, the sound of gunfire had returned to the basement, and Darren, his face once more bathed in the light of the screen, was deeply engrossed in the serious business of killing people.

What had Ludgrove thought Zak had seen that made him delete all those files from his computer? The files had to be somewhere, and Zak strongly suspected they had something to do with all this. The question of how to find them occupied him all the way back up to the seventh floor and Hendricks's messy desk. He found Hendricks himself carefully arranging his coat on the back of his chair. He didn't notice Zak until he spoke. 'All sorted.'

Hendricks jumped, and looked a bit flustered, first at Zak, then at the coat. He glanced around conspiratorially. 'Oldest journalist's trick in the book,' he whispered. 'Pop your coat on the back of your chair, everyone thinks you must be in the office somewhere. Just off for a spot of . . . well, Mum's the word, eh, Harry m'boy? Hold the fort here, there's a good fellow . . .'

'Liquid lunch, Rodney?' a female journalist with a black bob asked slyly on her way to the Ladies.

A mixture of outrage and embarrassment crossed Hendricks's face. He opened his mouth to protest, then clamped it firmly shut again.

'I'll stay here, Mr Hendricks,' Zak said, doing his best not to smile. 'Finish logging the sparrows. I'll be fine.'

'That's the spirit, Harry m'boy. That's the spirit.' Hendricks shuffled off in the direction of the lift while Zak took a seat. He confidently predicted that his boss wouldn't be back for a good couple of hours.

That should give him ample time to do some snooping.

He looked over his shoulder to see Hendricks waiting for the lift. But something else caught his eye too. It was Ludgrove. He was standing six or seven metres from Harry's boss, next to a water cooler and slightly concealed by a tall pot plant. Zak's line of sight was blocked, but he could still just catch the look in Ludgrove's eyes as he stared at Hendricks. It was a look of deep suspicion, and absolute hatred.

The lift arrived and Hendricks stepped in. Before the lift doors could close, however, Ludgrove was there, slipping inside more deftly than Zak would have suspected of somebody with his lumbering, brutish frame. As the doors hissed shut, he felt suddenly uneasy. If Ludgrove suspected Zak of something, he might think Hendricks was involved. He could easily try to beat some non-existent information out of the bumbling old nature-notes editor, and as Zak well knew, Ludgrove had form. He shot across the open-plan office, ignoring the strange looks from the startled journalists working at their desks. By the time he reached the lift, he could see that it had already reached the sixth floor. The stairwell was to his right. He ran towards it and hurtled down all seven flights, four steps at a time.

He was sweating when he emerged into the

reception area, but he was just in time. The lift doors opened. Zak wasn't quite sure what he expected to see – now that he was down here it seemed unlikely that Ludgrove would have done anything untoward on the actual premises of the *Daily Post* – but although Hendricks looked uncomfortable, he also looked unharmed. Zak lowered his head and stepped behind a pillar as the two men emerged. With relief he saw Hendricks leave the building, while Ludgrove walked up to the reception desk and started talking to the receptionist.

That relief soon fell away.

Hendricks had barely stepped out of the *Daily Post* building when Ludgrove broke off his conversation with the receptionist. She looked rather confused as he walked away from her and left the building. Through the glass frontage, Zak could see Hendricks walking west along Delfont Street, Ludgrove following him at a distance of about thirty metres. Zak hurried to the exit and joined the convoy, following Ludgrove at a similar distance.

He wished Raf and Gabs were with him. They had spent many a windswept afternoon on the island practising tracking techniques, but there was the world of difference between identifying the prints of wild animals and trailing a fully alert human being in an urban environment. Extra eyes would have been invaluable. Trailing someone who would recognize you if you got eyes on was hard. Get too close, you risk being seen. Not close enough and it was easy to lose your quarry. Zak *really* didn't want that to happen, although he couldn't have said why. Just that vague sense that if Ludgrove caught up with Hendricks, something bad would happen, and it might well be Zak's fault.

But there was no Gabs. No Raf. Just him. He concentrated hard on the job in hand.

The streets were not as busy as they might have been. Hendricks had stepped out early, and as it was only just past twelve very few of the local office workers were out on their lunch break. It was busy enough, however. Zak found himself zigzagging across the pavement to stop the oncoming pedestrians blocking his line of sight on Ludgrove. His target turned left at the end of Delfont Street. For ten seconds, as Zak sprinted to the street corner, both Hendricks and Ludgrove were out of view. He picked them out again as he turned the corner. About thirty metres up ahead, Hendricks was approaching a pub. Zak expected him to enter it for his liquid lunch, but to his mild surprise he walked straight on, seemingly unaware that he had two people following him.

Five minutes passed. Or maybe ten. Zak wasn't

keeping track of time, just of Hendricks and Ludgrove. When Hendricks crossed to the other side of the road using a zebra crossing, both Ludgrove and Zak risked the busy road – a taxi beeped at him, but Ludgrove seemed too intent on following Hendricks to look back and notice him. A right turn, and then another left. Zak didn't know where they were or where they were going. Not to the pub, clearly. The road ahead forked; they bore to the right and, twenty metres along this road, Hendricks took a sharp turn.

Ludgrove stopped. Zak did the same. He was breathing heavily, not through lack of fitness, but through anxiety. He didn't know what was happening, but it didn't feel good. But he saw why Ludgrove had stopped. The road into which Hendricks had turned was a dead end.

Zak stood with his back pressed against the red brick of a three-storey-high terraced building. Ludgrove was loitering by a pillar box, clearly deciding whether to follow his quarry or not. It took at least thirty seconds for him to decide to continue. Zak followed gingerly. When he saw Ludgrove stop and stare at the beginning of the road, he crossed the street again so he could share his view, albeit from a slightly greater distance.

Zak shared Ludgrove's obvious confusion. The mews was indeed a dead end. There were no roads leading off it, nor were there any doors on either side. A few cars were parked at a handful of parking meters, but apart from that there was no sign of anything. Including Hendricks. Where on earth could he have got to?

Suddenly, Ludgrove stormed down the street. He started looking underneath and behind cars and, when he found nothing, his frustration clearly got the better of him. He kicked the chassis of a grey Mercedes, and the blow echoed against the high walls of the mews. Zak allowed himself a smile. Bumbling old Hendricks probably had no idea he was being followed, but he'd managed to give Ludgrove the slip anyway.

And then, without warning, Ludgrove turned.

It was almost as if he knew Zak was there. Their gazes locked and an angry sneer curled onto Ludgrove's lips. He frowned, hunched his shoulders and started striding towards him.

For a moment, Zak considered standing his ground, but then he heard Gabs's voice in his head. '*Remember, sweetie, sometimes your legs are better friends than your fists.*'

From the look on Ludgrove's face – a deep frown, an angry sneer, a wildness in the eyes – Zak reckoned this was one of those times.

He ran.

1500hrs

A young woman with shoulder-length white-blonde hair and a grim-faced man were keeping very still. When you're conducting surveillance, movement is your worst enemy.

The location Gabs and Raf were watching was extremely ordinary: a terraced house, number 6 Galsheils Avenue, Tottenham, London. Their CR-V was parked directly outside. It had been simplicity itself to find out that this was where Ludgrove lived. 'His mother died eight years ago,' Michael had briefed them. 'Left him the house. Wife walked out on him last July. Domestic violence. He lives alone now. While young Zak has his eye on him, his house would be a good place to start snooping, don't you think?'

'I do hate that word,' Gabs had sighed.

Discovering a safe place from which to conduct the surveillance had been more complex. But not impossible, since Gabs and Raf had access to the kind of information most people would find it very difficult to come by. So it was that they had discovered that the occupant of number three, almost exactly opposite, was a Mrs Enid Sears, who lived alone but was currently in hospital having a hip replacement. The front bedroom of her deserted house was the perfect place from which to keep tabs on Ludgrove's place, and breaking in through the back way had been simple.

'Anything?' Raf asked.

Gabs gave a barely perceptible shake of her head.

'We've been watching for an hour. I say we go in,' Raf commented.

Under normal circumstances, an hour was nothing. They had both been on stakeouts that lasted days, and in far less comfortable surroundings than Mrs Sears's bedroom. But these were not normal circumstances. Michael's instructions had been very clear. *Check that there's no suspicious activity first. If anybody goes in or out of the house, I want to know who they are. If there's nothing, force an entry and see if you find anything incriminating . . .*

Gabs stepped away from the scope mounted on a tripod that she had trained at number six. Without speaking, she and Raf left the bedroom, and then the house.

Gaining access was easy. Raf was skilled with his tension tools and picked the lock in a matter of seconds. As they entered the house, both Raf and Gabs pulled their handguns before closing the door behind them.

The house was of a similar age to the Puzzle Master's, and a similar layout. Raf held back as Gabs stepped forward into the kitchen, ready to offer covering fire if needed. Nothing to report. She entered the front room. Ditto.

Raf gave an enquiring glance up the stairs. Gabs nodded. She moved up first, keeping her gun held high towards the landing. It was dark here. Dark and very quiet, the only sound the creaking of the floorboards underneath their feet.

And the sudden opening of the door downstairs . . .

Raf and Gabs froze. They heard something clattering.

Silence again.

Very slowly, they turned, gripping their handguns firmly. Raf led the way as they retraced their steps along the hallway, taking extra care to tread lightly and avoid the creaking. At the end of the hallway, they stopped. Raf held up three fingers of his free hand.

Two fingers.

One finger.

In a single movement they swung round to the top of the stairs, aiming their guns back down towards the hallway and the front door.

They froze again, shocked motionless.

The door was open. Standing quite still in the frame was the figure of a man. It was impossible to tell what he looked like, because his face was covered with an old-fashioned gas mask. He resembled a figure from the distant past. A ghost.

But he wasn't a ghost. He was very real.

Two seconds passed before Raf shouted, '*GET ON THE FLOOR WITH YOUR HANDS ON YOUR HEAD. NOW!*'

The figure didn't move.

'*GET ON THE FLOOR WITH YOUR HANDS ON YOUR HEAD, OTHERWISE I FIRE!*'

'Raf,' Gabs said sharply. 'Look.'

She pointed to a step halfway up the staircase. There was something there. It resembled a small canister, with a valve at one end. Now that they had noticed it, they could both hear a faint hissing from the valve.

And there was an acrid smell in the air.

'*Get . . . back . . .*' Raf breathed. But suddenly his voice sounded woozy. He staggered slightly at the top of the stairs. Gabs did the same. Her gun arm dropped. Her knees felt weak.

They fell at the same time, tumbling heavily down the stairs into an unconscious heap on the hallway floor.

14

TILT SWITCH

1905hrs

'Ludgrove's up to something,' Zak said. 'I'm certain of it. I know the NY Hero thing doesn't add up to much, but why would he delete those files from his computer? Maybe he'd been looking at dodgy websites – you know, there are plenty of people out there who think the 9/11 bombers in New York were heroes . . . where are we going, anyway?'

They were in a car, heading north. Michael had kept their 1900hrs RV at the Knightsbridge flat, but had done little more than walk in, greet Zak with a nod, then usher him wordlessly down to a red VW Polo parked in a nearby street. The car itself was shabby, and Zak understood why that was. To remain unnoticed, the last thing you wanted was a flash, ostentatious vehicle. When Raf had first abducted him from Acacia Avenue the day he became Agent 21, he'd used an old Post Office van. The red Polo was the same kind of vehicle. Unremarkable in every respect.

Well, *almost* every respect. Clipped into a mobile phone cradle was a small tablet computer. It showed a map of London, on which two red dots glowed around the Cricklewood area. This was more than an ordinary satnav.

Michael cut into a line of traffic as he headed up Park Lane. A black cab beeped angrily. Michael didn't even blink. An uncomfortable feeling grew in Zak's stomach. He had spent an awkward afternoon at the newspaper offices, doggedly logging sparrows, but Ludgrove had not reappeared. Nor Hendricks, until just before five p.m. when he had jovially breathed whisky fumes over him whilst patting him on the back for his endeavours with the sparrow log. Now, though, his intuition told him that something was very, very wrong.

'Michael, where are we going? What's happened?' he ventured.

His handler didn't take his eyes off the road. 'Gabriella and Raphael have missed three check-in calls, as well as the RV,' he said quietly.

The feeling in Zak's stomach turned to cold dread.

'What do you mean?'

Michael ignored that question, but pointed at the tablet computer. 'The map shows the location of their phones. We're going to find them.'

Zak swallowed hard. 'We should get some backup,' he said.

'*No!*'

'Why not?'

Michael breathed deeply. 'Our involvement here is a secret to everyone except those at the highest level of the security services,' he said. 'If something has happened to Gabriella and Raphael, it could mean that this secrecy has been compromised. I can't risk letting anybody know what we're doing.' Finally he glanced in Zak's direction. 'Do you still have your weapon?'

Zak shook his head. The little snubnose was back in the flat, safely locked away in a metal cabinet.

'Glove compartment,' Michael said. 'Locked and loaded.'

Zak opened the glove department. His eyes widened. He recognized the contours of a Browning Hi-Power. It had a suppressor fitted to the barrel in order to deaden the sound, and a telescopic sight attached to the top. A serious piece of kit, and the sight of it made his mouth dry. He knew perfectly well that under ordinary circumstances Michael would never expect him to wield a weapon like that in public. But these weren't ordinary circumstances. Two of their number were missing. That was unacceptable.

He closed the glove compartment and stared straight ahead. The traffic on the Edgware Road up ahead was clear. A little panel on the bottom left corner of the tablet gave their ETA.

Fifteen minutes.

Michael stopped the car fifty metres short of their destination, outside a boarded-up house in a shabby residential street. He tapped the tablet and a satellite map of the area appeared. He zoomed in. The dots appeared to originate from a large, square building on a street parallel to this one. It looked like a warehouse.

'There's a bag for your weapon in the back seat,' Michael told Zak. 'When you get to the warehouse, you'll see the main entrance on the western side. I'll take care of that. I want you to skirt round to the eastern side.' Another tap, and the schematics of the building came up. It was just one big room, with two windows on this eastern side. 'Cover me as I enter. If you see anybody with a weapon, shoot to wound. We need information, not corpses.'

'What if I miss them?' Zak asked. He instantly

regretted the question. Michael gave him a piercing look.

'Don't do that,' he said. 'Might I suggest that you go first? Individuals attract less attention than groups, wouldn't you say?'

Zak nodded. He reopened the glove compartment, removed the weapon and hid it in a battered canvas bag he found scrunched up on the back seat. Then he exited the car and started walking briskly down the road.

A crescent moon had appeared in the misty evening sky. Zak's senses were on high alert. He passed several houses where loud music was thumping from the window, and felt as though he could make out every beat. Two young men approached, wearing hoodies and bling. They gave him an aggressive look – did one of them glance at the canvas bag carrying the weapon? – but Zak walked past them with confidence. He was aware of their every movement, even of the sweat dripping down the side of one of their faces. If anyone tried anything, he would be on top of his game. Nothing was going to stop him from locating Raf and Gabs.

At the end of the street he looked over his shoulder. Michael was following. He had adopted the hunch of an old man, and looked strangely anonymous as he closed the gap between them.

He turned left, past a graffitied wall, and left again. The warehouse was thirty metres ahead of him.

Zak could instantly see that it had been deserted for a while. It was about twenty metres square and surrounded by a wire fence that had deteriorated through neglect and malicious damage. Zak stepped towards it without hesitation, his eyes scanning the surrounding area for signs of anything unusual. The warehouse was only a single storey, and he saw no sign of movement on the roof. The road that led to it had cars parked on either side. The doors of some of them were open, and more loud music was thumping from them as gangs of youths congregated in groups of four or five. Zak felt their eyes on him as he passed, and it crossed his mind that he and Michael were approaching this warehouse without a great deal of care.

It didn't matter. If someone had Gabs and Raf, there was no time to lose.

Up ahead there was a section where the fencing had been knocked down. Zak stepped across it, and over the bundle of barbed wire still attached to the top edge. The main entrance to the warehouse was ten metres away, but Zak didn't head towards it. As Michael had instructed, he skirted round the edge of the building to the eastern side. Before he turned the corner, he looked back again. Michael had straightened out and he was walking with grim purpose towards the warehouse.

Now that he was on the eastern side, Zak had nobody to overlook him – just a high brick wall that formed a narrow alley between itself and the warehouse. As Michael had predicted, there were indeed two large windows that looked into the warehouse. They clearly hadn't been cleaned for years. As Zak looked through them, he could barely see anything inside through the protective mesh, itself looking like it hadn't been maintained for years. A single big room, maybe? A table in the middle? It was instantly obvious that he would have to smash this window and bust the mesh if he had any chance of covering Michael as he entered.

He pulled his weapon from its bag, then looked left and right. Nothing. He raised the weapon and, with a short, forceful jab, smashed the butt against the window. It cracked and splintered. A second jab and the glass shattered. As the shards tinkled to the floor, Zak forced the rusting old mesh and immediately spun the weapon the right way round, raising the sight to his right eye. He panned left and right, scanning the room under the sight's magnification, his finger resting lightly on the trigger. Ready to fire.

Everything he saw sickened him.

There was indeed a table in the middle of the otherwise empty warehouse. Two mobile phones were sitting on it, side by side. Zak recognized them, of course. It was like they were mocking him, sitting there alone, without their owners.

He panned towards the door and upwards. There was something taped to the ceiling.

Lots of things.

Small packets connected with wires.

Just like he'd seen in the ceiling cavity of the hospital.

His skin prickled with fear. He did everything he could to keep his hand steady as his sights followed a wire that led from the ceiling, down the far wall, over one of the hinges of the door and towards the handle.

A lever handle. The type you press down to open the door.

But it had been tampered with. Big time.

It took a couple of seconds for Zak to realize what he was looking at through the magnification of his gun scope. Taped to the underside of the door handle was a glass test tube, the kind of thing you could find in any kid's chemistry set. The tube had a cork bung at one end, from which two wires protruded. The ends of each wire were visible inside the tube. But the test tube contained something else. Sitting at the rounded end was a metal ball bearing.

A sick wave of panic crashed over Zak as he realized what it was. A tilt switch. As soon as somebody opened the door handle from the other side, the ball bearing would roll toward the wires, completing the circuit, and then . . .

Bang.

It all happened so quickly.

Zak heard himself screaming as loud as he could: 'MICHAEL, DON'T OPEN THE DOOR!'

But it was too late. The handle was moving.

There was nothing else Zak could have done. Even as the ball bearing started to roll, he fixed the test tube in the cross hairs of his sight.

He only had a single shot.

A single chance to blow the switch.

He fired.

There was a dull, knocking sound as the round flew from the suppressed barrel. The jolt of the weapon meant that Zak lost sight of the test tube for a fraction of a second, but he pulled it back in time to see three things.

The glass had shattered.

The ball bearing was falling to the floor.

And splinters were flying as the round ripped a hole in the wooden door.

Zak held his breath as five seconds passed in dreadful silence.

The door started to creak open. Slowly at first, but with increasing speed. Horrified, Zak saw a figure tumble into the room. Shoulder-length grey hair. A shocked expression. Both hands covering his stomach.

Michael hadn't even hit the floor by the time Zak had jumped through the shattered window. He sprinted across the room towards his handler just as his body thumped onto the hard concrete. He rolled Michael onto his back – the old man was shaking violently, and sweating – only to see an alarming quantity of blood oozing from behind his hands covering his stomach.

Instantly, Zak pulled out his own phone and dialled 999. He barked their location down the phone, screaming at the operator that somebody had been shot, then turned his attention back to Michael himself. His handler was dreadfully pale, and his lips were blue. He coughed weakly, and then whispered Zak's name, and a single word: '*Go!*'

Zak shook his head and tried to put pressure on the wound. 'I'm staying,' he said. 'The ambulance will be here any second.'

Michael's eyes fell closed, and he spoke again, obviously with great effort. 'If the police . . . find you here . . . questioning . . . too long . . . you have to go . . . stop Ludgrove . . . stop . . .. the third . . . device . . .'

'I'm staying with you,' Zak insisted through gritted teeth. *There was so much blood* . . .

Michael opened his eyes, obviously with difficulty. 'Order, Zak . . .' he breathed. 'Find Ludgrove . . . go . . . *now!*'

As if to underline his instruction, sirens blared in the distance. And deep down, Zak knew Michael was right. He couldn't get taken in by the police. They'd force him to explain things that couldn't be explained. They'd force him to waste time.

Time he didn't have.

'I'm going to find Raf and Gabs,' he whispered. 'And I'm *going* to stop this guy.'

But Michael had lost consciousness. Blood was pooling around his body. And the sirens were growing louder.

Zak stood up, ran to the window and exited. With his weapon stashed back in the bag, he strode away from the warehouse as calmly as he could.

He could hear the sirens arriving from the south. He walked north. Michael's instruction was ringing in his ears.

Find Ludgrove . . . go . . . now!

15

HANGMAN

Zak didn't start running until he was out of sight of the warehouse. But then he ran like hell.

His mind was churning, and so was his stomach. 'Find Ludgrove,' he whispered to himself, a desperate attempt to keep his thoughts straight. '*Find Ludgrove...*' But no matter how he tried, he couldn't get the image out of his mind of the blood seeping from Michael's stomach wound. It had been a bullet from Zak's gun that had injured him. If he died, Zak knew he would carry the guilt for ever. But there was a stronger, more urgent emotion even than that: rising panic that something bad – something *really* bad – had happened to Raf and Gabs. Clearly the warehouse had been a trap, designed to kill whoever went looking for Zak's Guardian Angels. A little voice in his head told him that, given

203

this was the case, the chances of Raf and Gabs being kept alive were tiny. Almost non-existent. But he didn't listen to that voice. He couldn't. He *had* to believe they were still alive. He *had* to . . .

Find Ludgrove . . .

But what was he supposed to do when he found him? How could he do this by himself? Who would he even report to?

He wiped the hot, angry tears that were collecting in his eyes with the back of his hand. *Get a grip*, he told himself. *You can't do anything in this state. You're drawing attention to yourself when you need to be invisible. Lives depend on it.*

He realized he'd been walking without knowing where he was headed. He found himself outside a McDonald's on Cricklewood Broadway. It was growing dark now, but still quite warm. Zak noticed a splash of Michael's blood on his right hand so he ducked into McDonald's to wash it off.

The washrooms were in the basement. They looked deserted, apart from one of five cubicles – the third along – that was locked. He placed the canvas bag on the back edge of a sink, behind the taps, and started washing the blood from his hand. The water ran pink, but the stain was stubborn and he had to scratch at it with the nails of his left hand.

He heard the chain in the occupied cubicle flush

and a man emerged. He was in his thirties and his thinning hair was cropped close. He stood at the sink next to Zak to wash his hands and Zak saw him glance down. The man's eyes widened as he saw the blood. They flickered towards the canvas bag. To his horror Zak saw that the dull end of the suppressor was poking out from the corner of the bag.

The man yanked his gaze away from the gun, immediately stopped washing his hands and left the washrooms without drying them. Zak cursed under his breath. He'd seen the gun. There was no doubt that he would raise the alarm. Grabbing the canvas bag, he left the washroom and jogged up the stairs. Back in the main area of the restaurant, he took a moment to scan the room. Most of the tables were occupied – there were perhaps fifty people in here – and he quickly identified the guy from the wash-room talking to a uniformed security man by one of the big flip-top bins approximately eight metres to his five o'clock. Almost as a reflex action, his eyes picked out three CCTV cameras on the ceiling. One was pointing in his direction. It had him. No doubt.

Distance to the exit: fifteen metres. It meant passing right by the security man. No point waiting. He paced quickly towards the door.

'That's him,' the man hissed as he passed. Zak felt the security guy shrink away as he upped his pace.

Five metres to the door.

'Stop that boy! He's got a gun!'

A sudden silence in the restaurant. Zak sprinted. He hurled himself against the door, which opened outwards onto the street. Once he was outside, he sprinted again. All he could think of was getting a good distance between himself and the McDonald's. He allowed himself one glance backwards. The security guy was outside the restaurant, looking left and right, but he clearly couldn't see Zak amid the other pedestrians. Zak slowed down to a steady walk, so that he didn't draw any more attention to himself. But even though he was walking calmly, his mind was in turmoil. What was he going to do? Michael had set him an impossible task. He couldn't go to the police – they'd dismiss him as a fantasist, or worse. And right now, he couldn't risk being stopped by anyone, not with the kind of luggage he was carrying. He was alone. Totally alone. And although London should have felt more secure to him than Mexico or Angola, it didn't. And how had he turned into the kind of person who could terrify a whole McDonald's? He needed to get back to the flat in Knightsbridge. There at least he felt safe. Or at least, safer.

The blue and white frontage of Cricklewood Broadway station loomed up ahead. Two armed police officers guarded its entrance. Remembering how he had been searched at Victoria, Zak immediately dismissed the idea of trying to use public transport. If anyone found the Browning, he'd be flat on the floor with his hands on his head. Instead, he walked straight past, studiously avoiding eye contact with the officers.

It was about two minutes later that he saw a black cab coming his way. He flagged it down and the driver pulled up alongside him, winding down his window as he did so. 'Where you going, son?'

'Knightsbridge,' Zak replied.

'Gotta charge you double to go into central London, what with these bomb scares and all.'

'Fine,' Zak said shortly. He climbed into the back of the cab.

'Ain't you got school tomorrow, son?' the driver asked as he pulled out into the traffic.

'It's closed,' Zak replied automatically. 'Because of the . . . you know . . . attacks.'

The answer seemed to satisfy the cab driver.

'Know what I think?' the driver said, accelerating down Cricklewood Broadway. He didn't wait for an answer. 'I think it's that Al-Qaeda doing it. Old Bin Liner might be dead, but they still got a load of nutters want to make their mark.'

'Yeah,' Zak nodded absently. 'Probably.' But he

didn't agree. The features of Ludgrove rose in his mind. The sour-faced journalist hardly seemed like a wannabe Al-Qaeda operative. He was, however, Zak's only lead.

The cab crawled through the traffic back into central London. The driver switched on the radio – some call-in show – and Zak zoned out as the DJ and his guests made increasingly wild speculations about the events of the past few days. He stared out of the window as they passed through Paddington. Everywhere he looked there was heightened security: ordinary police, armed police and, as they entered further into the centre, soldiers in camouflage gear with weapons strapped across their chest. Zak found himself focusing on the faces of these men who were there to protect the capital. They looked far from sure of themselves. Hardly surprising. They were trying to stop something that hadn't happened yet. They didn't know what, or when. Or even *if*.

Looking up, he saw two aircraft circling low in the night sky. Zak couldn't make out what they were, but he suspected they were also to do with the heightened security. A strange thought crossed his mind: in a city under attack from an unknown bomber, in the air was probably the safest place to be.

An urgent voice on the radio brought him back

to the here and now. It was the DJ of the call-in show. 'Reports are coming in of an incident in the Westminster area of London. Our understanding is that there has *not* been another explosion, but a police spokesman is advising the public to avoid the area at all costs.'

Zak looked out of the window again to get his bearings. They were heading down Park Lane, towards Hyde Park Corner. 'Can you take me there?' he asked the cabbie.

'Where, son?'

'Westminster.'

'You got a bleedin' death wish, mate? Course I ain't takin' you to Westminster. Didn't you hear what they just said?'

Zak grabbed his wallet from inside his coat and pulled out a bundle of notes which he waved in the cabbie's direction.

'Forget it, son,' the cabbie insisted. 'I don't want to be the richest man in the cemetery. I'll take you to Knightsbridge like you asked, but that's it.'

They had arrived at Hyde Park Corner now. Time check: 21.05. Zak made a sudden decision. 'Let me out here,' he said.

The cab driver looked at him like he was mad. But then he shrugged, and pulled over on the eastern edge of Hyde Park Corner. Zak pushed a handful of notes in his direction and the driver's eyes widened slightly when he realized that his passenger had paid him far more than he was supposed to, but by that time Zak was slamming the cab door shut. He hitched the canvas bag holding his weapon up onto his right shoulder, and sprinted in the direction of Constitution Hill.

The road leading down towards Buckingham Palace was clogged with stationary traffic. Some drivers were even standing by their cars, looking up ahead to see what the holdup was. Zak hurtled past them, towards the palace that was bathed in light. He was half aware of the Union Jack flying, but the best part of his attention was on speed. When he reached the Queen Victoria Memorial, standing proud on the roundabout in front of the palace, he headed south, then turned left down Birdcage Walk.

His lungs were burning again. The hard corners of his weapon dug uncomfortably into his ribs. The closer he came to Parliament Square, the more clearly he heard a cacophony of sirens up ahead. The traffic was at a standstill here too, so much so that most drivers had switched off their engines and were looking ahead with furrowed brows. The beeping horns of the more impatient drivers joined the blare of the sirens. For Zak, it was the sound of panic, and it made fear rise in his gut.

What was going on? *What was happening?*

The road veered slightly to the right. Parliament Square came into view: immobile traffic, grand buildings, statues, and of course Big Ben. The clock face glowed pale yellow in the night, like a second moon. Twenty-five past nine. Zak ran towards it. As he entered Parliament Square he was able to cross the road easily because of the log-jammed traffic, and he could see that whatever was causing the hold-up was centred around Westminster Bridge. There were four or five police cars there, and the bridge itself had been closed off.

Zak didn't know what it was that made him run towards the bridge. Just a vague, uneasy sense that he needed to see what was going on here. That it was relevant, somehow, to him. As he grew closer to the bridge, though, he realized there was no hope of getting onto it. There were several policeman keeping the cordon, and they were letting nobody past. Zak peered towards the flashing lights of the police cars. They were parked halfway along the bridge, and he could just make out the shape of figures leaning over the edge to look down towards the river below.

He felt a chill. What were they looking at? What had happened?

Zak looked to his ten o'clock. A small crowd had

gathered on the bank of the river and they were looking up at the bridge. He ran towards them, his sense of unease growing. For some reason he avoided looking up until he had joined the crowd.

What he saw when he finally gazed towards the bridge both sickened and astonished him.

There was a rope hanging from the railings. And, at the end of the rope, a figure.

Unbidden, the faces of Raf and Gabs rose in his mind. A cold sickness gnawed at him.

He looked around. The crowd was concentrated in a small area about twenty metres from the bridge. He could be undisturbed if he walked just a bit further along the bank. He did so, then crouched down behind a green litter bin and felt inside his bag. Blindly, he unclipped the sight from the top of his weapon before quickly zipping the bag up again. He held the sight up to his right eye, and directed it at the bridge. He squinted as the flashing blue neon of one of the police cars filled his sight, then lowered his aim in line with the hanging body.

It was a man. Zak saw that immediately because he was still wearing his suit. He directed his line of vision onto the hanged man's face and fine-tuned the focusing. Because of the distance, his field of view was small and it was a struggle to maintain a steady enough hand to keep the man's face in view.

It was a deeply unpleasant sight. The tongue was lolling from one side of the mouth, and the whole face was a rictus mask of terror. Zak found himself checking the hair colour. Dark. Briefly, he felt a wave of relief. If he had dark hair, this man could not be Raf.

The relief was short-lived. As Zak turned his full attention back to the man's face, he realized he knew who it was.

He let the sight fall, blinked at the hanging silhouette, then returned the sight to his eye to make sure he wasn't mistaken.

He *wasn't* mistaken.

Sirens continued to ring in his ears. The horns continued to beep. Zak gaped open-mouthed at the bridge, trying to work out what it all meant.

Trying to work out why, and how, the corpse currently hanging from the railings of Westminster Bridge could possibly be Joshua Ludgrove, chief defence correspondent of the *Daily Post*, all-round bad egg and the only person Zak had in the frame for the devastating attacks on London, and the chaos that had ensued.

As Zak reeled in confusion, not far away – only a few miles – a man was busy. It was dark down here. As dark as night. *Darker* than night, in fact. With the total absence of light – he didn't even illuminate his watch, so he could only guess that it was now about 9.30 p.m. – he was obliged to survey his prisoners using a pair of fourth-generation night-vision goggles. The NV goggles included an infra-red torch, which cast its light – invisible to the human eye – in a fan shape ahead of him, lighting everything up with a hazy green glow. But the prisoners, when they woke up, would not see anything. If he remained still, they would probably not even know he was there.

He sat, and watched, and waited. The only noise was the scurrying of rats, but he'd grown used to those hairy creatures with their long, greasy tails in the time he had spent here.

So much time. Such a lot of planning.

It was the woman who woke first. She had white-blonde hair which glowed pale in the NV. Her chin drooped onto her chest and her hair fell forward. As she roused herself, she lifted her head up and stared blindly into the darkness, her eyeballs glinting strangely in the infra-red beam of which she was totally unaware. She tried to stand, and it was only then she realized her hands were tied behind her back, although she had no way of knowing that they were also tied to an iron ring protruding from the clammy stone wall.

'Raf?' she whispered, her voice dry and hoarse. 'Raf, are you there?'

He turned his attention to the man. He was stirring too, and at the sound of the woman's voice, he groaned. 'Gabs?' he rasped.

Good. So now he knew their names. That was a start.

'What happened?' Gabs asked. 'All I remember . . . the stairs . . .'

'We were gassed,' said the man called Raf.

'That's why I feel so sick,' Gabs muttered. 'I think someone hit me on the head too. I can feel a welt.'

It was true. He had hit them on the head. He didn't quite know why, because the gas had been enough to keep them unconscious for several hours. It was just a sudden moment of anger towards these two people who had obviously been close to ruining everything.

Both Raf and Gabs tried – without success – to free themselves from their ropes. He knew their struggles would be in vain, but it amused him to watch them anyway. They struggled for about thirty seconds before falling still again.

'Who was he?' Gabs breathed. 'The man in the mask, I mean.'

Raf shrugged in the darkness. 'Who knows. Ludgrove, I suppose. It was his house, and he's our number one suspect.' He suddenly swore under his breath and yanked at the rope again. 'How do we get out again? Where *is* this place.'

'It doesn't smell too good,' Gabs observed, 'and it's damp. How long do you think we've been out?'

At the word 'Ludgrove', he had allowed himself a cold smile. He'd worried that they'd been on to him. But just as he himself had figured, the defence correspondent would be a likely suspect if anyone figured out the crossword clues. And so it had turned out. He needn't have been concerned that he himself could have been a suspect. And Ludgrove, easily overcome when arriving home, was no longer any problem. He smiled at the memory. Another corpse on a rope. In plain sight too. But his problem now was these two. Perhaps he ought to kill them right now. He had a gun at his side and it would be a simple task. His prisoners would be dead before they even knew what was happening.

No, he told himself. He had longed for this for too long to risk carelessness at this late stage. And he wanted the information they could give him about the final fly in his ointment . . .

'You may wish to know,' he said in a quiet voice – he saw his two prisoners' faces look sharply in his direction – 'You may wish to know that it is a moment's work for me to snuff out your lives.'

A tense silence. The man called Raf spoke. 'You don't have to do this,' he breathed. 'We can help you. It doesn't have to end the way you think it might—'

'Please,' he cut in, his voice dripping contempt, 'spare me the negotiation techniques. I'm probably as well-trained in them as you are.'

'I doubt that, sweetie,' the girl called Gabs murmured.

'I saw you entering the house of that fool who calls himself the Puzzle Master. You had someone else with you. A boy, perhaps. I want his name, and I want to know where I can find him.'

Even through the night vision, he could see their eyes tighten. Their lips, however, remained firmly closed.

He allowed the question to hang there for thirty seconds, before tutting dramatically in the darkness. 'You will tell me,' he said, in a sing-song voice that he knew unnerved people. 'Sooner or later, you will tell me.'

They looked stubbornly ahead, but said nothing. It was time, he thought to himself, to allow them a little light. He pushed the NV goggles up onto his forehead and then, from a bag by his feet, he removed a powerful Maglite torch. He aimed at the the two prisoners and switched on.

They hissed as the light burned their retinas and they clamped them shut. It took a minute or so for them to open their eyes wide again. He didn't worry that they would be able to see him because he was behind the light and they were dazzled.

'Look around,' he breathed. 'Take in your surroundings.' He shone the torch up and down, left and right, and felt a certain amount of pride at the scene that it revealed.

They were in a low-ceilinged space – he saw no reason to tell them exactly where it was – and they were surrounded by ten crates, all packed full of C4 plastic explosive, all linked, one to the other, by a metal wire. On top of one of the crates was a tiny detonator, much like the one he had planted in the hospital. It consisted of a digital clock face (as yet unlit), a small circuit board (of his own devising) and a space for a single AA battery. He pulled such a battery from his pocket and stepped towards the detonator. Holding the battery an inch above the detonator, he looked over at his two prisoners. 'My advice,' he whispered, 'is to sit very, *very* still.'

He gave it a couple of seconds for the instruction to sink in, then slotted the battery into place.

The clock lit up and immediately started counting down.

06:00:00
05:59:59
05:59:58

Everything was set.

He switched off his torch and re-engaged the NV goggles. The clock glowed brightly, but he was more interested in his prisoners just now. 'For your information,' he whispered, 'you are both sitting on a pressure pad. If you move off it, all ten of our little boxes will go kaboom. I'll come back when you've had time to think things over, and I'll allow you one more chance to tell me who else is on my trail. If you give me the information, I shall consider helping you leave the blast site. If not . . . let's just say that your family won't need to go to the expense of buying a box to bury you in.'

'I've got a better idea, sweetie.' The woman's voice rang clearly in the darkness. 'Seeing as we're never going to tell you anything, why don't I just jump up right now and take you with us?'

He gave a short, sardonic laugh. 'By all means,' he said, calling her bluff. 'I've been looking forward to my grand finale for some time now. Oh, forgive me, you don't know where we are! Still, it hardly matters if you're about to blow yourself up, does it?'

As he spoke, he stepped backwards. He could still

see the prisoners' faces staring blindly, and he could tell from their expressions that they weren't about to move anywhere.

He turned his back on them and retreated, padding through the dark, dingy tunnels he had got to know so well.

16

EVORGDUL

It was only by chance that Zak found himself outside New Scotland Yard. He'd been striding blindly, sweat oozing from every pore of his body, his mind turning over. The sight of Scotland Yard, however, forced him to stop and clear his head. There wasn't time to be confused. He needed to establish what he knew. To separate the significant from the insignificant. And he needed to do it now.

Someone was planting bombs in London, and advertising them in cryptic ways. Why advertise them? He didn't know. Two had already exploded, and there was likely to be a third. Someone had called the Puzzle Master from the offices of the *Daily Post*. Until now, Ludgrove was the prime suspect, but now he was dead. Suicide? Unlikely. Zak had met him only briefly, but he hadn't seemed like a man about to kill himself. A murder unconnected to the bombings? Zak didn't think so. That would be too much of a coincidence.

All sorts of possibilities rose in his brain. Perhaps Ludgrove had been in league with somebody else, but had fallen out with his accomplice. Perhaps the journalist had stumbled upon something, and his very public execution was a warning to anybody else who might be on the trail of the bomber. That thought made Zak's face harden. If the bomber thought he was going to scare Zak away like that, he had another think coming. Not with Raf and Gabs missing, and Michael in hospital. He wondered briefly, too, if Malcolm Mann had survived his gunshot wound. A boy he had failed to protect . . .

One thing was sure. Somehow, and for some reason, Ludgrove must be at the centre of all this.

It wouldn't take the police long to identify the corpse hanging from Westminster Bridge. When that happened, they'd be swarming round his house like bees round a hive. Zak had to get there first, search the place, try to break into Ludgrove's home computer before the police did. He screwed up his eyes and furrowed his brow. When Michael had been briefing them back in the Knightsbridge flat, Gabs had read out Ludgrove's address. Where was it? *Where was it?*

Suddenly he opened his eyes. He saw another black cab coming his way and flagged it down. Almost before the vehicle came to a halt he was jumping into the back and shouting urgently at the driver. 'Six Galsheils Avenue,' he said. 'Tottenham.'

2327hrs
Galsheils Avenue was deserted. As the cab drove away, Zak strained his ears for the sound of sirens. He examined the vehicles parked on either side of the road as he walked towards number six, checking that none of them were in fact covert surveillance posts. He neither saw, nor heard, anything unusual.

Zak didn't have Raf's skill at picking locks. His method of entry was more blunt. At the end of Galsheils Avenue was the entrance to an alleyway that ran behind the houses. Zak hurried along it, counting down until he came to number six. He scrambled over the garden fence, through the high grass of the unkempt garden, and up to the house. With a sharp jab of his elbow, he smashed a hole into the French doors that led out onto the garden. He waited a minute to check he hadn't alerted any of the neighbours to his presence, but seconds after that he was in.

He stood for a moment in the darkness of a musty-smelling dining room. What was he after?

What was he looking for? He decided that his first goal had to be searching for Ludgrove's computer. He stole down the hallway, checking the kitchen and the front room as he went – no sign of a desktop or laptop – then found himself at the bottom of the stairs.

Two things caught his eye in the lamplight that streamed in through the frosted glass of the front door. The first was a canister, about halfway up the stairs. It looked not unlike a grenade, but he could see that it was spent because the pin had been pulled and the safety lever released. It obviously *wasn't* a grenade, though, because the building was intact.

And on the first step, there was something that brought a twist to his stomach. A diamond hairpin in the shape of a star.

Zak's eyes went flat. He picked it up, held it to the light and saw that it was smeared with blood. 'Ow!' he breathed suddenly, realizing he had cut himself. The edges of the star were razor sharp. Trust Gabs to own a piece of jewellery like that. Beautiful *and* dangerous, the same as her.

He put the hairpin in his pocket and climbed the stairs.

The floorboards on the landing creaked but Zak concentrated on speed rather than stealth. He had to be out of here before the police arrived, as they surely would. Ludgrove had a home office at the front of the house and here, on a table surrounded by piles of papers and newspaper cuttings, was an old desktop computer. Zak sat down in front of it and turned it on. It seemed to take an age to boot up – the hard drive sounded old and clunky – and as soon as the operating system had booted, Zak was presented with his next hurdle.

Enter password. Warning: incorrect password will trigger immediate system erase.

Zak cursed. It meant he only had a single guess. Then he remembered: he also had something to go on.

Zak removed his phone from his pocket. He swiped the screen, entered his passcode and navigated to his videos. The last piece of footage he had taken had been in the basement of the *Daily Post* as Darren the IT guy logged on to Ludgrove's work system. Was it possible that Ludgrove used the same password for both systems? There was only one way to find out.

Zak replayed the video paying close attention to the IT guy's fingers. He was touch-typing as he entered the password, and as far as Zak could tell it was eight characters long. He watched the footage again, paying close attention to which finger typed each character. He grabbed a scrap of paper and a pencil that were lying on the desk in front of him and, for each character, scribbled down either L or R depending on which hand the IT guy had used, and a number from one to five, depending on which finger.

L3
L2
R4
L2
L2
L3
R2
R4

Once his list was complete he laid his fingers across the middle of the keyboard. He had learned how to touch-type at school in what seemed like another life. He remembered a rather drab teacher telling him that it was like learning a bike – you never forgot once you had learned – and that he'd be glad that he'd taken the time to master it. Zak had rather doubted it at the time. Now he had to concede that his teacher had been right, but not for the reasons anyone could have imagined at the time . . .

The IT guy had inputted the first character of the

password with the third finger of his left hand. Zak looked at the keyboard, then wrote down the possible keys it could have been: 3 4 E D C. He did the same thing for the remaining characters until he had a grid of all the possible combinations.

```
L3   3   4   E   D   C
L2   5   6   R   T   F   G   V   B
R4   0   O   L   .
L2   5   6   R   T   F   G   V   B
L2   5   6   R   T   F   G   V   B
L3   3   4   E   D   C   S
R2   7   U   J   M
R4   0   O   L   .
```

He stared at the characters, knowing that he needed to choose one from each row but unable to see any kind of pattern or keyword. Perhaps Ludgrove's password was just a random string of letters. If so, Zak had no chance. He only had one attempt to get the right password. He began to panic.

But then, as he stared at the paper in the glow of the computer screen, he saw it. Could it really be that simple?

He circled one letter of each row.

```
L3   3   4   (E)   D   C   S
L2   5   6   R   T   F   G   (V)   B
R4   0   (O)   L   .
L2   5   6   (R)   T   F   G   V   B
L2   5   6   R   T   F   (G)   V   B
L3   3   4   E   (D)   C   S
R2   7   (U)   J   M
R4   0   O   (L)   .
```

Then he read the highlighted letters from the bottom up: LUDGROVE.

Could the password really be his name spelled backwards? Could it really be that simple? Zak breathed deeply, then carefully typed it in: EVORGDUL

He pressed enter.

The screen went blank.

And then it flickered into life. He was in.

There was no time to congratulate himself. The police could be here at any moment. Zak's first instinct was to check the list of previously opened documents. It was empty. He cursed silently, and repeated his curse when he saw that the folder labelled 'My Documents' was empty. He didn't have *time* to trawl the whole hard drive looking for information. *Think*, he told himself. *What else do you know?*

He opened up a search window and typed in NY HERO.

No results.

He tried to stay calm, to put his mind back to the offices of the *Daily Post*. He hadn't been sure that the final 'O' hadn't been a 'D'. He'd put that from his mind because NY HERD meant nothing to him. But now he typed these letters into the search window and pressed enter.

Result.

A link to a single document appeared. Zak double-clicked it, and for the next minute, he did nothing but read.

The document was entitled 'Richard Sonny Herder' – NY HERD, he immediately saw, was simply part of that name. The name meant nothing to Zak, at least not until he read through what appeared to be an article Ludgrove was writing.

On 18 June 1973, the British Army committed one of its least glorious, and least known, travesties of justice. Richard 'Sonny' Herder was, along with his brother Lee, a highly accomplished bomb-disposal expert working in Northern Ireland during one of the worst periods of the Troubles. Rumours have abounded among Dick Herder's contemporaries about the manner of his death. Why did the Ministry of Defence go out of its way to cover up Herder's death and the circumstances surrounding the car bomb that caused it? What is the truth behind the subsequent disappearance of his brother Lee? These secrets have remained buried for forty years. Now, after many months of research, and having spoken to eye witnesses who were there, I can reveal the full, shameful truth of what happened that day. Dick Herder's death was caused not by his own carelessness, but because he was ordered to defuse a device that he himself had declared unsafe to approach. His story is a shocking indictment of the British Army, and the way it treats the memory of its fallen.

But it is more than that. It is a story of deception, intrigue and subterfuge . . .

Zak wanted to read on, but his attention was suddenly ripped away from the text on the screen. The window of this first-floor office looked out onto the road. And on the road, bathing the study in flashing neon light, were three police cars. He could hear men shouting instructions to each other.

He stood up so abruptly that his chair toppled backwards. He grabbed the canvas bag containing his weapon and hurtled along the landing and down the stairs. There were shadows behind the frosted glass of the front door. As he reached the bottom of the stairs there was a sudden, shocking bang from the doorway. The door rattled in its frame and an image fell into Zak's head of the police officers on the other side forcing it open with a pneumatic battering ram. He knew it wouldn't survive another strike, so he didn't hang around. Seconds later he burst out of the French doors, sprinted the length of the garden and scrambled over the wooden fence at the bottom.

It was only as his feet slammed against the ground that he saw them: three officers, one of them holding an Alsatian on a lead, running down the alleyway in his direction. The dog barked; one of the officers shouted. They were no more than twenty metres away, and closing. Paralysed by panic, Zak stared helpless at them for a second.

The dog barked again.

'Get on the ground! *Get on the ground!*'

Zak snapped out of his hesitation. A couple of metres behind him were two green wheelie bins. He scrambled on top of them, then hurled himself over the brick wall that formed one side of the alleyway. He fell heavily onto tarmac on the other side, but quickly scrambled to his feet again. He was in the car park of a modern red-brick church. It was deserted at this time of night, so he pelted across it, past the church itself and out on to a busy main road.

He ran for thirty metres, dodging the occasional pedestrian, until he came to a bus stop. The doors of a red, single-decker bus were just closing as Zak ran up to them. He hammered on the door and shouted at the top of his voice: '*Please, let me on!*' For a sickening moment he thought the driver was ignoring him, but then there was a hiss as the doors concertina'd open.

Zak slapped his Oyster card – in the name of Harry Gold – against the reader and scurried down the bus, looking over his shoulder and half expecting to see armed police bearing down on him.

But then the doors hissed closed. As the bus drove away, he staggered to the very end, feeling the glances of the other passengers keenly. It may have been a trick of the light, but he thought he saw a uniformed man with a dog appear at a distance of about twenty metres.

Or maybe it was just a pedestrian. Zak had no way of knowing as he took a seat, placing the canvas bag carefully on his lap. He tried to recall everything he had read on Ludgrove's computer. *Richard 'Sonny' Herder . . . 'Dick' to his friends . . . died in a bomb blast 18 June 1973.*

18 June 1973 . . .

Zak looked at his watch. 1159hrs. With a kind of sick anticipation he watched the seconds tick down.

0000hrs. 18 June.

His mouth went dry. He closed his eyes. His mind was a confused pot of loose ends and half theories, but one fact burned brightly. Today was the fortieth anniversary of Herder's death. Ludgrove had been writing a story about that death, and if the terrible events of the past few days were linked somehow to that bomb blast of forty years ago, there was no reason not to think that the third bomb could be scheduled for today.

But Ludgrove was dead. He could give him no answers now.

Zak sat there with his eyes shut, thinking carefully about what his next move had to be.

18 JUNE

17

THE GRAVEYARD SHIFT

Midnight.

Normally a good, quiet time to be working in a hospital. Not tonight. Tonight it felt as if there were *no* good times to be working in a hospital. Tonight it really did feel like the graveyard shift.

First the underground bomb. Dr Cooper had been on call as the gruesomely injured bodies had been carried into surgery. Three of them had died under his care, and as a doctor it didn't matter how many lives you saved, it was those you lost that you always remembered.

Then the children's hospital. There wasn't a single member of staff here who hadn't watched the footage on television of its destruction. And there wasn't a single member of staff who didn't wonder if *their* place of work was going to be next.

Dr Cooper was no exception. He had come to work today against his better judgement, and hadn't been surprised to learn that thirty per cent of the staff had called in 'sick'. In a way he didn't mind: it meant the day had been so busy that he barely had time to worry about terrorist attacks. Now, though, as he stood in the bright lights of the operating theatre, his face covered by a mask, his hands by skintight latex gloves, he found his mind wandering. He had been appalled by the news of that poor man hanging from Westminster Bridge, and he was appalled now by the sight of the patient in the operating theatre. The man on the table was an elderly man, in his late sixties, perhaps, although his physique was of a man half that age. Perhaps it was this that had enabled him to survive his gun wound, so far. He had shoulder-length grey hair and Dr Cooper had disapprovingly noticed a smell of tobacco about him. He had no name, at least none that anyone had been able to find. No relative had come forward to claim him. There was just an ID card that had made the hospital security staff jumpy. Dr Cooper had had to explain in no uncertain terms to a faceless bureaucrat who seemed to have appeared from nowhere that his patient absolutely couldn't be moved to another hospital if he had any chance of living. What had happened to the patient,

Cooper had no idea. He had just been found, bleeding half to death, by the police after an anonymous tip-off, and rushed into A&E immediately. That meant *someone* knew what had happened, but they were keeping quiet.

Bad things were happening in London. This was one of them. And it felt like the whole capital was holding its breath, waiting to see what was next.

'Scalpel,' he said.

The wound was bad. The bullet had punctured the man's stomach lining and caused a massive amount of internal bleeding. This man was on the brink of death and it looked like being the graveyard shift in more ways than one. Dr Cooper's eyes flickered towards one of the screens surrounding the operating table. His patient's vital signs were weak. Low blood pressure. Low pulse. He exchanged a nervous glance with the anaesthetist. 'It's not looking good,' he said. The anaesthetist shook his head.

The scalpel was sharp. It cut with ease through the skin of the old man, and the thin layer of fat beneath. As the blade sliced through his flesh, the man's blood pressure dropped a couple of points. Dr Cooper carried on with the procedure nonetheless.

It was pitch dark, but it was not entirely silent. The pitter-patter and squeaking of rodents was all around them, and more than once both Raf and Gabs had felt something brush against them. The thought of being surrounded by rats was repulsive, but they barely noticed them. All their attention was focused on the glowing countdown of the digital clock.

04:57:56
04:57:55
04:57:54

'Where do you think we are?' Gabs breathed. It was the first time either of them had spoken for an hour.

'Underground,' Raf sniffed. 'That seems to be his *modus operandi*. The first device was in a tube tunnel, the second one in the basement of the hospital.' A pause. 'Are you OK?'

'Not really.'

They sat in silence for a few more minutes, neither of them daring to move in case they disturbed the pressure plates beneath them.

'We're not going to tell him, right? About Zak, I mean.' Gabs sounded a little fearful that Raf would disagree.

'Of course not,' he said firmly.

'He *will* leave us here to die,' she said, her voice

no louder than the rodent squeaks around her.

'I know.' Raf sniffed. 'You remember the lesson we were giving him? About Enigma and the Coventry bomb?'

'Of course.'

'Works both ways. Maybe we could save ourselves by giving up Zak's identity. But he and Michael are the only ones with a chance of stopping this maniac. If we have to die to help them . . .' His voice trailed off.

'I never thought this was how it would end.'

'It hasn't ended yet,' said Raf, but he didn't sound all that convinced.

'What can we do?'

Another pause.

'I don't know,' Raf said. 'I guess we just wait here and hope that Zak and Michael come up with something.'

'They haven't got long,' Gabs whispered.

The clock continued to count.

04:55:04
04:55:03
04:55:02

Zak sat, anonymous, at the back of the bus. The other passengers were eyeing him suspiciously, but then they seemed to be eyeing *everyone* suspiciously. There was that kind of mood in the capital tonight. Zak ignored them. He had other things on his mind. Like the fact that with the death of Joshua Ludgrove, all his leads had dried up. Breaking into the journalist's computer had gleaned nothing. All he knew was that Ludgrove had been investigating the death of some soldier forty years ago to the day. It was old news, and try though he might, he could see no connection, other than today's date, with the events of the past few days.

And yet, Ludgrove was dead. Murdered. Why?

It crossed Zak's mind that he should talk it over with his Guardian Angels, but that one thought made him feel coldly nauseous as he remembered that two of them were missing and one of them was gravely wounded, possibly dead . . . Panic welled up in him again. His eyes darted around as he desperately tried to think what to do.

'What's the matter with you, lad? You don't look well.' An old man in a peaked cap was sitting opposite him, looking genuinely concerned.

'I . . . just . . . it's nothing,' Zak mumbled.

'Worried about all these goings on, are you? You aren't the only one, lad. But they'll find him, whoever's doing it all. They always do, in the end. You see on telly, that fella hanging off the helicopter when the hospital went down? Nobody got a look at his face, did they, but at least we know we've got blokes like that looking after us.' He sniffed. 'Cowardly way to do war if you ask me. Planting bombs, killing innocent people. When I was in the Forces . . .'

Zak blinked. 'What did you say?'

'I said, cowardly way to do war . . .'

But Zak was remembering someone else who'd said a similar thing. *They're cowards, aren't they, people who plant bombs. I don't like cowards.*

Malcolm. With everything else that had happened, he'd almost forgotten about the strange boy he'd broken out of the secure hospital just a couple of days ago. It had all started with Malcolm, but Zak had barely spoken to him. Perhaps he was conscious now. If so, perhaps he knew more than he had told.

Before he knew it, Zak was muttering an apology at the old man who had started reminiscing about the war, and was walking up the aisle towards the exit doors. He peered through the bus window to see that it had started to rain again. Through the rain he saw the familiar sight of, among others, a neon Coca-Cola sign. Piccadilly Circus. He rang the bell to halt the bus at the next stop, and moments later was jumping out onto the pavement of Lower Regent Street.

He needed to head south, but something stopped him. Time check: 0022hrs. He had an idea.

Zak ran north instead, sprinting across the road to the north side of Piccadilly where he found what he wanted: a newspaper stall selling the first editions of tomorrow's papers. He grabbed a copy of the *Daily Post* and glanced briefly at the headline – 'London Under Attack' – before rustling through it until he found the crossword. Standing there in the soaking wet, the rain smearing the ink on the pages of the newspaper, he stared at the empty grid. The clues were challenging; on the previous two crosswords he'd had the advantage of a completed grid. Now he had nothing.

It meant he needed Malcolm's help more than ever. He rolled up the newspaper, tucked it under his jacket, and ran south towards Pall Mall, his trainers slapping in the wet as he went. He turned east and ran towards the river, suddenly glad to be operating on familiar territory. Knowing his way around the London streets saved a lot of time. And time was crucial.

He remembered that the entrance to the hospital where Malcolm was being treated was just off Victoria Embankment. By the time he was standing outside that inconspicuous 'car park', he was wet through. He stood for a moment, listening to the distant sirens that told a story of high security in the capital. Then he ran down the ramp, past an unmanned barrier to find himself in that empty basement. Last time he'd been here, the double doors at the far end had been open, paramedics waiting to receive the wounded Malcolm. Now they were closed, and all was silent. The only sign that this was a hospital was a single stretcher bed parked outside the double doors with a sheet draped over its sides, and a metal bin, taller than Zak, which said 'Medical Waste Only'.

Zak stepped over to the double doors and pressed gingerly at the security bar. It was locked, and he cursed. To the right of the door was a numeric key-pad – he hadn't noticed it last time he was here – but without the access code it might as well have been a big iron chain. Zak had no idea how he was going to get inside. He looked around the car park. There was no other exit.

He felt stupid standing there, not knowing what to do or how to get inside. His wet clothes had turned cold, and he was shivering as he listened to the noise of the traffic outside. Was it him, or did it sound as though a siren was getting closer?

And closer . . .

He looked up the ramp of the car park and saw a sudden flash of an ambulance's light.

He had to lose the gun. He had a plan, but the weapon would hold him back. He quickly removed the magazine then threw the weapon into the metal bin, before chucking the magazine in separately. He'd hardly made it safe, but at least it wasn't going to go off by accident, and nobody would think to look for a weapon in a bin full of old bandages. Now that he'd rid himself of the firearm, he quickly ran to the stretcher bed and climbed underneath it. He grabbed the underside of the frame at one end and pulled himself upwards. His biceps and stomach muscles hardened as he felt for a place on the frame to support his feet. After a few seconds, he just managed to clip his toes into a gap in the frame. It was a strain to hang on, but he was committed now: the siren had stopped, the lights were still flashing and he could hear the ambulance screech to a halt next to him.

Zak kept his breathing slow and shallow and concentrated on stopping his strained limbs shaking the stretcher bed. The sheet hid him from sight but also blocked his view. He could hear a commotion next to him, though, and within seconds he felt a weight – presumably a person – being placed on the bed. 'Move,' barked a voice. Zak heard someone tapping the keypad, then a scraping sound as the double doors opened up. 'Get him into the lift,' said the voice. Suddenly Zak was on the move.

'We're losing him,' a tense voice said. They were in the lift now, and the doors were hissing shut. Zak wasn't sure how much longer he could hold on as the lift moved upwards, coming to a halt about ten seconds later. As the doors opened again, the same voice shouted: 'Get him into theatre, *now*!'

They were moving again, quickly along a corridor. Zak's hands were slipping. They crashed through a set of double doors. 'Get him onto the operating table!' yet another voice ordered. Zak sensed the weight being lifted from the stretcher. 'Get that bed out of here. We need the space.'

He was wheeled out again. Zak heard footsteps disappearing, then silence.

He wanted to hold on a bit longer, but it wasn't an option. It felt like every muscle in his torso and legs were shrieking at him. Easing himself down onto the floor he looked both ways along the corridor – it was about twenty metres in length – to check nobody was coming. The coast was clear, so he crept out from underneath the bed.

The sheet that had been hiding him was stained red. Zak ignored that. He needed to find Malcolm's room, and fast. He was right outside the operating theatre and could see, through the Perspex panels in the doors, a great deal of activity in there. He headed down the corridor, where he could see the doors to four more rooms, two on either side.

He struck gold with the first one. It looked like a surgeons' scrubbing-up area – lockers, sinks, alcohol gels for cleaning hands. Next to the lockers was a shelf full of neatly folded doctors' gowns. Zak pulled one of the light green gowns over his wet clothes, then covered his hair with a fabric hat and his face with a surgeon's mask. The disguise wouldn't stand up to a robust inspection, but it was better than nothing. He left the room and was immediately glad he'd dressed up – two doctors were jogging in his direction, clearly rushing to get to the operating theatre. They barely looked at Zak as they passed.

He continued along the corridor. The next door on his right looked onto an empty ward. On his left, some kind of common room, also empty, with a TV in the corner showing footage of Westminster Bridge. The second door on the right had no glass panels, but it had something none of the others did: a security guard, sitting outside. He had a newspaper folded in front of him, and seemed to be filling in the crossword. Zak ignored the irony and, without even thinking about what would happen if he messed this up, drew himself up to his full height, put on an air of confidence he didn't really feel, and approached.

'Any sound from him?' he asked the security guard, grateful that the mask muffled his voice.

'Sleeping like a baby,' the guard said without even looking up. 'Wish I was too.'

'I'll check on him.'

The security guard nodded and continued to fill in his crossword.

It was dark in this room, but from the light of the corridor, Zak could see that it contained just a single bed. He closed the door and, using his phone as a torch, crept into the room.

Bingo.

Malcolm was asleep this time, propped up by a number of large pillows but, astonishingly given how bad his wound had been, free of any kind of medical apparatus. A drip stand stood in one corner of the room, along with a blood-pressure machine, but neither were connected to his body. Even so, he looked frail, his face gaunt and white. The bed sheet covered only the lower part of his body while a large, sterile dressing was spread over most of his right shoulder. His breathing was shallow.

Zak held out his left palm, ready to cover Malcolm's mouth and muffle any sound of surprise when he woke him. He was just about to switch off the phone, however, when Malcolm's eyes suddenly pinged open.

Zak jumped, but Malcolm himself looked neither scared nor surprised to see him standing over him. He clearly recognized him, despite the darkness and Zak's surgeon's mask. With his good hand he reached out for his glasses and put them on.

'I want to leave,' he said.

Heavy footsteps outside the door. Zak froze. They faded away.

'You can't leave, Malcolm. You need to get better. You were badly injured.'

'It hurts,' Malcolm agreed. 'But you said you would help me get away.'

There was an awkward pause. Gambling that Malcolm wasn't about to raise the alarm, Zak pulled the mask off his face then sat down at a chair next to the bed. 'I worked it out,' he said. 'The crossword, I mean. The cipher. I couldn't have done that if you hadn't put me on the right track. Thank you. It saved a lot of lives'

'It was obvious,' Malcolm said. 'If *I* wanted to hide something, I would be more careful.'

Zak couldn't help a smile. 'I don't think *most* people would find it obvious, Malcolm.' And he thought: *But you're not like most people, are you?* 'How often do the doctors come in and see you?'

'In the daytime, every hour. At night, not so often.'

'Right. I haven't got long, Malcolm. I need your help. I think there's going to be another bomb, and I don't know where.'

'Nor do I,' Malcolm breathed.

'Does the name Richard "Sonny" Herder mean anything to you?'

The boy shook his head.

'Joshua Ludgrove?'

A blank look. 'Who are these people?'

'Dick Herder is some dead soldier from the seventies. Ludgrove worked at the *Daily Post*, the newspaper that published the crosswords.'

'Why do you say worked? Has he been sacked?'

Yeah, Zak thought. *Permanently.*

'He's dead. Murdered, sometime this evening. He was investigating the death of this Herder guy forty years ago.' Zak shook his head. 'Maybe it's got nothing to do with anything. The guy who normally sets the crosswords is dead too. Someone tried to force him into printing three replacement crosswords. We've decoded two of them.' He pulled out today's *Daily Post* from under his jacket. 'I think this could be the third. Can you solve it?'

'Of course,' Malcolm said, like it was a stupid question. 'But why should I?'

Zak blinked in the darkness. 'This bomber,' he

replied carefully, 'is trying to massacre innocent people.'

'People die,' Malcolm interrupted. 'All the time.'

'For God's sake, Malcolm,' Zak breathed. 'He blew up a *children's* hospital. Don't you want to help catch him?'

Malcolm sneered. 'Nobody wants to help me. They want to throw me into a secure hospital and throw away the key.'

The words *for your own good* danced on Zak's lips as he remembered the gunmen at Harrington Secure Hospital, and how lucky Malcolm was to be alive. But something told him that kind of argument wasn't going to wash with Malcolm. He didn't think the way other people thought.

'I can get you out of here,' he said. Malcolm looked at him sharply. 'Not now,' Zak said hastily. 'You're too weak and you need to recover. But I've done it once and I can do it again. You know I can, right?'

For a moment Malcolm didn't reply. Then he nodded.

'But I'll only do it,' Zak said, 'if we stop the third bomb. If not . . .' Zak gave him a severe look. 'Well, I hope you like hospital food.'

Their eyes locked in the darkness. Then, with a painful wince, Malcolm took the newspaper from

Zak and, in the light of the mobile phone, Zak saw his eyes scanning the clues beneath the crossword grid.

'Do you need a pencil?' Zak asked.

'Shhh . . .' was the only reply.

There was a minute's silence. Malcolm's eyes flickered back and forth. Finally he laid the newspaper down in front of him. 'There are no messages here,' he said.

'Are you sure?'

'Of course I'm sure. If there was a message, I would see it.' There was no hint of doubt in his voice. 'Maybe the bomber knows you have discovered his code. He would stop using it then, wouldn't he?'

Zak gave a short nod. He felt like hope was draining from him. He recovered the newspaper from Malcolm's bed and started folding it up. 'I have to go,' he said.

'Where?'

Good question. Where *could* he go? What could he *do?* Hide out in the Knightsbridge flat? Get out of London?

Or maybe, go back to work. The *Daily Post* was still his best lead. In the absence of any better idea, he should get back there. Do some more snooping. He heard Gabs's voice in his head. *I do wish he'd stop using that word . . . it sounds so uncouth.* A sudden anger filled him. His only friends were missing and he had done *nothing* to find them. And now he was out of ideas. But if he couldn't find a solution, and soon, people would be likely to *die . . .* He stood up. 'I'm going to spend a day talking birds with a boring man called Rodney Hendricks,' he said bitterly. 'Nice knowing you, Malcolm.' He strode towards the door.

'Wait.'

'I can't. If they find me here . . .'

'*Wait!*' Zak heard the boy shuffle up in his stretcher bed. 'What did you just say?'

'I'm going back to the paper, see what I can dig up.'

'You *didn't* say that. You said . . . *Rodney Hendricks . . .*'

'Yeah. So?'

'Don't you see?' Malcolm sounded almost contemptuous. 'It's obvious, isn't it?'

'*What's* obvious.' Zak was losing patience.

'Did you say you had a pencil?'

Zak blinked in the darkness. 'Yeah,' he said, finally. He pulled a pencil from his jacket pocket and, still lighting his way with his phone, returned to Malcolm's bed.

'Give me the paper,' Malcolm said. Zak handed

over the paper and pencil and watched as, in the glow of the phone, Malcolm scribbled the name of Rodney Hendricks in the blank margin of the front page.

'Don't you *see*?' he repeated.

Zak shook his head. 'See *what*?'

One by one, Malcolm started crossing out the letters in Hendricks's name, then writing each letter in a new space next to it as he did so. The D first. Then the I. Then the C.

And gradually, a new name appeared.

DICK SONNY HERDER.

'It's an anagram,' Malcolm said. 'I can always spot them. Rodney Hendricks is a fake name. It's obvious.' He peered sharply through his glasses. 'Didn't you say Richard Herder was dead?'

'Yeah,' Zak breathed. He could hardly believe what Malcolm had just revealed. That it had been there, under his nose, all the time. 'Yeah, he's dead.'

'So, why would this Hendricks guy take his name . . . ?'

All of a sudden, the pieces were falling into place. He recalled two lines from Ludgrove's article. *Why did the Ministry of Defence go out of its way to cover up Herder's death and the circumstances surrounding the car bomb that caused it? What is the truth behind the subsequent disappearance of his brother Lee?*

The brothers were bomb-disposal experts. But surely, anybody who is expert at defusing a bomb, would be an expert at constructing one too. 'Rodney Hendricks isn't Richard Herder,' he breathed, improvising slightly but knowing with a strange clarity that he was on the right track. 'He's his brother, Lee. And he's about to take his revenge – today, on the anniversary of his brother's death. I've got to find him . . . stop him . . . now . . .'

He was already standing up and heading for the door.

But suddenly it opened.

A figure stood there, dressed in doctor's scrubs but Zak recognized him instantly. Black hair, slicked back. Flat nose. Weapon in his right hand. It was one of the two men he had fired at outside Harrington Secure Hospital. One of the two men who had come to kill Malcolm. And who had just killed the security guard sitting outside, whose body was slumped in his chair, his blood spattered all around.

'GET OUT OF BED,' Zak roared, even as he hurled himself at the impostor. They both fell into a scrambled heap in the corridor outside Malcolm's room.

Zak heard the pop of a silenced pistol.

18

THE LONG-TAILED SHRIKE

The man was short, squat and burly. He was obviously immensely strong. Zak had only managed to floor him because he'd had the element of surprise. With both of them in a heap on the ground, he felt the round from his adversary's gun whip past his right ear. With all the force he could muster, he swiped one arm against the man's gun hand. The weapon clattered a couple of metres along the corridor.

Zak didn't go after it. He scrambled to his feet and lunged back into Malcolm's room, shutting the door behind him. There was a twist lock underneath the handle. Zak turned it and heard a thin clunk. It wasn't much of a lock. It wouldn't hold anybody for long. He switched the light on.

Malcolm was sitting up in bed. He didn't look

scared. Bemused, if anything. 'Is he going to kill us?' he asked, with the innocence of a small child.

'No,' Zak said, his teeth gritted. 'He isn't.'

As he spoke, there was the pop of another gun-shot from outside. The door splintered, just a couple of centimetres from the lock. They had seconds before the gunman was inside. Another gunshot. Another splinter. They had seconds.

'Can you walk?' Zak demanded.

'I think so,' said Malcolm. He winced as he carefully swung his legs over the side of the hospital bed. Zak looked around the room. He needed a weapon. There was nothing. In the end, his eyes fell on a glass jug of water by Malcolm's bed.

A third gunshot. The hole by the lock was the size of Zak's fist now. He grabbed the water jug and emptied it over Malcolm's bed. 'Stand by the door,' he told the boy. 'By the handle, not the hinges.'

Malcolm nodded and, one hand clutching the bandage over his shoulder, took up position by the door.

A thud. The door rattled in its frame. The gunman was kicking it in. Zak could tell it wasn't going to hold. Clutching the water jug with his left hand, he stepped over to the door, unlocked it with his right and then yanked it open.

The gunman was taking another kick. As the

door opened, however, he tumbled into the room. Zak smashed the glass jug down on his head. It shattered. The man fell, bleeding from his scalp. Unconscious. Zak seized the gun from his hand and turned to Malcolm, who looked like he was watching an interesting TV programme.

'We need to get out of here,' Zak said. 'There could be others like him, but the hospital staff will probably try to stop us. Don't be surprised by anything I do or say – I promise I won't hurt any of them, or you.'

Malcolm nodded, then winced again. Together, they stepped out into the corridor. Zak tried not to look at the gruesome sight of the dead security man's body.

At first, he thought they might get away unnoticed, that the sound of the gun had sent all the hospital staff into hiding. He soon realized that wasn't the case. Three security guards appeared at the end of the corridor and they started running towards Zak and Malcolm. Zak didn't hesitate – he raised the gun into the air and fired at the ceiling. The security guards stopped as a shower of plaster fell to the ground and Zak placed the weapon against the back of Malcolm's skull.

'*Get on the ground with your hands on your head, or I'll shoot!*' he roared, his voice only slightly muffled by the mask.

The guards looked nervously at each other. Then they hit the ground.

'Walk,' Zak hissed at Malcolm.

There was a strange silence as they edged down the corridor. As they passed the men on the ground Zak lowered his gun in their direction to stop them from getting brave. Once they had cleared them, he told Malcolm to up his pace. Thirty seconds later they were at the top of a stairwell.

Voices echoing down below. Zak fired another shot. It hit the ceiling, debris rained down loudly and even Malcolm, who seemed immune to fright, jumped at the noise. Zak repeated his instruction to get on the ground by bellowing down the stairwell. They descended to find four doctors lying down, and the exit door that led out into the car park wide open.

'Outside. Now.'

Zak slammed the double doors as they exited. As an extra precaution, he fired a single shot at the key-pad that opened them. He didn't know if that would disable the doors, but it was worth a try. He turned to Malcolm. 'How are you doing?'

The boy's face was white. He looked very weak. But he nodded.

'We need to get to Knightsbridge. We'll be safe there. Do you think you can walk that far?'

For the first time, Malcolm looked uncertain. 'It *really* hurts,' he said.

'I know. I'll be able to give you something for the pain when we get there. But it's not safe for you here any more.'

Sirens. Approaching.

'We have to move.' Zak took off his jacket and helped Malcolm put his good arm through one of the sleeves while draping the other over his wounded shoulder. It wasn't much, but it helped disguise his plain white hospital pyjamas a little. Malcolm's slippers would get soaked in the rain, but there was nothing Zak could do about that. They just had to get to the flat as quickly as possible.

And then what? He didn't know.

They emerged onto Victoria Embankment to find the rain falling more heavily than ever. It was a blessing in disguise. At this time of night, there were few people about anyway, but with this rotten weather, the streets were almost clear. Visibility was poor. And even though they could hear the sound of police cars growing nearer, nobody stopped them as they shuffled off through the elements.

By the time they reached the safety and shelter of the Knightsbridge flat, they were soaked through and Malcolm was shaking alarmingly. Zak stripped the boy of his clothes and gave him towels to dry himself before he even thought about sorting himself out. In the bathroom he found a medicine cabinet. It was somewhat better stocked than the average first-aid kit. There were morphine injections and saline bags here, as well as sterile dressings and prescription painkillers. For a moment, Zak's hand hovered over the morphine, but then he rejected the idea. It was true that it would make Malcolm more comfortable, but it would also make him less sharp and Zak had a feeling he was going to need the boy's skills before the night was over. He took the painkillers and the dressing to where Malcolm was sitting quietly in the front room, looking out over the London skyline.

'Take these.' He handed Malcolm two tablets, and the boy swallowed them without complaint. 'I should change your dressing. It got very wet out there.'

Malcolm nodded his agreement and lowered the top of the white gown Zak had given him to wear. Carefully, Zak pulled away the adhesive strips that held the dressing to Malcolm's skin. The boy winced, but did not complain, as Zak revealed the full extent of his gunshot wound.

'You're lucky it didn't shatter a bone,' Zak said as he examined the surgeon's handiwork. The entry wound had been neatly sewn up, but the whole area was bruised and bloodshot, and the wound had started to weep a colourless plasma. Malcolm made occasional hisses of pain as Zak carefully applied a fresh dressing. Once the job was completed, he looked paler than ever. It was clear he needed more medical care than Zak had expertise to give him. It was equally clear that his life was in danger if anybody located him. That meant staying here, for now.

Zak checked the time. It was a little before 3 a.m. His thoughts turned towards Rodney Hendricks. Could it be true that this strange, dumpy little man with thick round glasses and a passion for sparrows could be behind the terror that had raged through London over the past few days? It seemed wildly improbable. Perhaps the anagram was just a fluke. A coincidence.

Zak hit the Internet. He Googled Richard Herder. He quickly identified plenty of people of that name, but they were all very much alive: one was an American real-estate agent, one was a schoolboy, one was a priest in Cornwall. Zak trawled through several pages, trying to find any reference to a former soldier with that name, but he found nothing. Until, that is, he clicked the Images tab.

He found it tucked away on the bottom of the fourth page of results. It was an old photograph, a clipping from a parish magazine of 1971. It showed two young men smiling for the camera, both smartly dressed in military uniform. The caption below read: '*Brothers Richard (left) and Lee (right) Herder, photographed on the day of their deployment to Northern Ireland.*'

Zak stared at the picture. They both looked so fresh-faced. Young. Eager to serve. For a moment, Zak couldn't take his eyes off the picture. The brother on the right had not yet grown a beard, or taken to wearing glasses. He did not yet have a paunch. But there was no doubt about it. Lee Herder was a young Rodney Hendricks.

Zak spun round to where Malcolm was sitting quietly. He had started to shiver again. 'Mate,' he said, 'are you absolutely sure there's nothing in that crossword? Nothing we've missed?'

'Show it to me again.'

Zak fetched the soggy newspaper and showed Malcolm the crossword. The boy's eyes flickered rapidly up and down as he examined the grid. 'Nothing,' he said after a minute. 'Trust me.'

Zak *did* trust him. But where did that leave them? Perhaps he'd got it wrong. Perhaps today was not the day that London should expect the third bomb. Somehow he didn't think so. Hendricks was un-hinged, and today – the anniversary of his brother's death – would be significant to him. Zak didn't know why he was planting these coded messages, but Hendricks surely knew by now that someone was on to him, because they had been able to evacuate the hospital before the second bomb detonated. Under those circumstances, it made sense that he had replaced the final crossword with an innocent one. But if so, perhaps he had planted his message elsewhere. And how did that dead-end mews fit into all of this? What was *that* all about? Was that why Ludgrove was dead?

'Give me the paper,' he breathed. Malcolm handed it over and Zak flicked through the pages until he reached the nature-notes column. It was tucked away in the bottom right-hand corner of a page towards the end of the newspaper, next to an unfunny cartoon and below an advert for mortgages. A passport photo-sized picture of Hendricks peered out from the page. Zak read the copy alongside it.

The Long-tailed Shrike. Quiet, graceful, powerful. Every person near Yarmouth will witness jaw-dropping, Xanadu-like tails, unbelievably splendid swooping and diving as flocks of this rare bird, seldom seen in the British Isles, swarm to the south coast of the United Kingdom . . .

'The long-tailed shrike,' he murmured. He remembered his morning in the newsroom less than twenty-four hours ago. The editor had insisted that Hendricks write a piece for today's paper on the effect the second bomb had had on the wildlife of the city. Hendricks had insisted that he wanted to write about this obscure bird, but then had appeared to back down. And yet, here it was, the article he had been so eager to print?

Why?

There could only be one reason.

Zak cursed under his breath. He should have known all along. Xanadu-like tails? A phrase like that didn't even make sense. Hendricks had to have put it in there for some other reason. He handed the newspaper to Malcolm. 'It's here,' he said.

'What do you mean?'

'The message. It's somewhere in this article. Hendricks insisted on printing something about the long-tailed shrike – it's a bird. Why would he care so much, if he's in the middle of a bombing campaign?'

Malcolm took the newspaper and looked at the article. His eyes started flickering again until, after about twenty seconds, they widened.

'I need a pen,' he said.

Zak grabbed a pencil and a pad from a nearby

desk and handed them to the pale-faced boy. Instantly he started writing.

L O N G T A I L E D S H R I K E

'What's the cipher?' Zak breathed.

Malcolm didn't answer. Instead, like the system of using the initial letters of down clues in the crosswords, he circled the first letters of the next sixteen words of the article, counting hyphenated words as just one word each. Zak tried to decode it in his head. *L=11, Q=16, add them together you get 27, which is a B . . .* But he was a thousand times slower than Malcolm, who was already writing down the decoded message on the pad in his thin, spidery writing.

He underlined the message once. Zak stared at it. Then he stared at Malcolm. Then he stared out over the London skyline.

'Are you sure it's right?' he asked Malcolm.

'I'm sure,' said the boy.

Zak closed his eyes and did everything he could to stem the panic rising in his gut. He opened them again and double-checked what Malcolm had written.

L O N G T A I L E D S H R I K E
B U C K I N G H A M P A L A C E

He blinked. His mouth went dry. They had discovered the location of the third bomb. If Zak was reading the signs right, the blast would happen today. And it could happen at any minute . . .

19

CHALKER MEWS

Raf and Gabs's abductor had returned.

'I trust the passing of a few hours has made the decision-making process a little easier for you,' he said. He shone the torch in the direction of the digital clock face, though he needn't have. They had been watching it glow in the dark for hours, silently willing time to slow down.

01:00:01
01:00:00
00:59:59

'You know what?' Gabs said. She was doing what she could to sound upbeat, but her voice rasped and she wasn't doing a very good job of it.

'Enlighten me,' said the man.

'We *have* come to a decision.'

'I'm delighted to hear it.'

'And our decision is,' Gabs continued, 'that we'd rather eat worms than tell a sicko like you anything.'

The man smiled. 'How ironic,' he said, a slight edge to his voice. 'Because in reality it is the worms that will be eating you in, oh, approximately fifty-nine minutes and thirty seconds. You won't be their only meal, of course, but you'll be their closest.'

'Not if—'

'QUIET!' he roared suddenly. And then, in a much milder voice, he continued, 'I understand your game. You wish to goad me into moving close to you. Then you hope to wrestle me onto the pressure pad and yourself off it. But rest assured, my dear lady, I won't allow that to happen.'

Gabs threw him a look of utter loathing, but the man seemed immune to it.

'Why?' Raf asked quietly.

'I beg your pardon?'

'Why are you doing this? What can you possibly hope to gain from all this slaughter?'

'Satisfaction!' the man snapped. 'After all these years!'

'All these years of what?' Raf's voice was measured and calm – a stark contrast to the bomber's, which was shrill and excitable.

'All these years of loneliness!'

'And you think killing people is going to earn you friends?'

The bomber spat in contempt. 'I don't *want* friends. My brother was my only friend, and he was taken from me years ago. I swore I would avenge him.' He looked upwards. 'And now I will.' He started to edge away from them, into the darkness.

'Tell me about your brother,' Raf persisted.

The bomber stopped. 'He was more of a man than you.'

'What was his name?'

'*What does it matter to you?*' the bomber hissed. But then, almost unable to stop himself, he said: 'His name was Richard.'

'He sounds like quite a guy,' Raf breathed.

'He deserved better.'

'What happened to him, mate?'

The question seemed to tip the bomber over the edge. 'You don't know what happened to him, because they covered it up!'

'Who covered it up?' Raf pressed.

'The army. The government. Everyone!' The bomber glanced at the clock ticking down. 00:58:03. It was almost as if he was deciding whether he had the time to tell his story. 'We were the best,' he said, whispering now and taking a step towards Raf and

Gabs. 'He taught me everything I knew about bomb disposal, but together we were the best.'

Another step forward.

'There was a car bomb. Northern Ireland. We knew it was too dangerous to defuse. We walked away. But some Rupert forced him into it. Said he'd get someone else in. Richard knew that if anyone else tried it, they'd die, so he went in.'

'That was brave,' said Raf.

'It was more than brave,' the bomber snapped. 'They should have given him a medal. A proper military funeral. They didn't. They wrote him out of history to keep it quiet.' A pause. 'But they're paying now.'

He was standing five metres from Raf.

'What's your name, mate?' Raf said.

'What does it matter?'

'It matters to me.'

'Fine,' the bomber said. 'Call me Rodney.' His voice changed suddenly. 'Rodney Hendricks,' he said in a self-mocking voice. 'Birds this, nature that . . . everyone thinks Rodney's a fool, but none of them saw through my little disguise. And birds can kill. Even something as insignificant as a little chaffinch.' He started laughing, as if at some private joke. If he noticed the glance Raf and Gabs gave each other, he made no sign of it.

'Rodney,' Raf said. 'Where are we? You might as well tell us, if we're going to die anyway.'

Hendricks stopped laughing. 'I found my way down here years ago,' he said. 'I've been planning this ever since but until now I had no funds to pursue my aims. That changed, and my little conflagration on the underground killed many people, while destroying the hospital was spectacular, but believe me, nobody will forget today.'

'Where are we, Rodney?' Raf repeated.

'Underneath the Palace.' He pointed at the ten crates of explosives. 'There's enough here to bring the building crumbling in on itself. My brother fought for Queen and country. They betrayed him, so what better way is there to avenge him?'

Hendricks was breathing deeply. There was excitement in his voice. He stood there for a moment, looking not at Raf and Gabs, but at the crates.

'Why the crosswords, Rodney? What made you want to send those coded messages.'

'Let's just say I needed to prove my worth to a wealthy patron whose aims coincide with my own. I have always wanted to avenge my brother, but I'm afraid terror costs money – money that I've never had, until now. Don't imagine for a moment that the British establishment has seen the end of me.

Quite the opposite. Once I have more funds at my disposal, the fun's *really* going to start.'

'And Richard?' Raf asked quietly. 'If he was here, what would he tell you to do?'

Hendricks looked sharply at him. 'What?'

'You heard me, Rodney? He was a soldier. A good one. Would *he* think this was fun? Would he would thank you for killing innocent people in his name? Do you think that's what he would want his legacy to be.'

'His legacy is what it is,' said Hendricks.

'But you can change it, Rodney. You can make him the hero you know he is. You understand that, don't you?'

The question hung in the air between them. Hendricks's breath became shorter. Quicker.

'Defuse the device, Rodney,' Raf whispered. 'Do it for Richard.'

Hendricks stared at him. Then he stared at the clock counting down.

It felt as if the world was holding its breath. Gab and Raf certainly were.

The bomber's lip curled. 'Impossible,' he breathed. 'Once it's primed, any attempt to defuse it will spark a detonation. And in any case, why would I think of allowing you to live. You two, the only people in the world who know my little secret.'

'Not the only ones, Rodney,' Gabs told him. 'Not for long. Our people have eyes at the *Daily Post*. It won't take them long to work it out.'

'I never told you I worked at the *Post*,' Hendricks shot back. And then, suddenly, his eyes widened. 'Harry Gold,' he breathed. He gave a mirthless laugh. 'Don't try to deny it, lady. I can see the way your jaw clenches, and how you refuse to catch my eye. It was stupid of me not to guess before. Why else would tedious, disregarded Rodney Hendricks be sent a work experience boy. Unless, of course, he was there to spy on him. Or on our erstwhile friend Ludgrove?' He smirked. 'You see how well I understand the way you think? Well, don't worry, my friends. I'll make short work of a kid like Harry. Just like I did with the Puzzle Master and Ludgrove himself.' He sneered. 'I see you are shocked. But remember, I was a soldier before I was a bomb-disposal expert. I was *taught* to kill. And Ludgrove was digging into the old story, beginning to discover my true identity. He had to go . . . As will young Harry.'

'Don't count on it, sweetie,' Gabs breathed.

But now Hendricks was receding into the darkness. Raf shouted at him: 'Hendricks! *Hendricks!*' But the bomber simply grinned at him and didn't reply. He switched off his torch. Everything went quiet, apart from the scurrying of the rats and the sound of Hendricks's receding footsteps. And everything went black apart from the blue glow around the digital display:

00:56:02
00:56:01
00:56:00

Zak felt almost paralysed. He needed to raise the alarm. But how? He heard Michael's voice in his head. *The authorities receive tip-offs galore, most of them from cranks and time-wasters. It's normally the case that genuine tip-offs can be confirmed by more than one source. That's the way intelligence-gathering works.* If Zak went to anybody and told them there was about to be a bomb blast at Buckingham Palace, and he knew because there was a secret message in a daily newspaper, chances were that he'd end up in Harrington Secure Hospital with Malcolm.

But he had to do something.

He paced the room, his face screwed up with concentration. Hendricks – or Lee Herder, to give him his real name – liked spectacular gestures. If he was going to hit Buckingham Palace, this wasn't going to be some feeble indoor fireworks display. It was going to be big. But surely such a place would be heavily guarded? Surely security would be tight? To lace Buckingham Palace with enough explosives to do the kind of damage Hendricks so clearly wanted to do was, if not impossible, surely unfeasibly difficult.

So how would he do it?

The answer came to him in a flash. *Underground.* That was the bomber's *modus operandi*. He'd planted the Pimlico bomb in an underground tunnel. He'd planted the hospital bomb in the basement. What if, somehow, he'd gained access to the area beneath Buckingham Palace?

'Oh my God . . .' Zak whispered.

'What?' Malcolm asked.

'I know what he's done. I know where the explosives are.'

'Where?'

But Zak didn't reply. Not directly. 'They need to evacuate the palace,' he said. 'Even if the Queen's not there, there must be any number of innocent people working in the building.' He swore under his breath. 'If only Michael was here. Or Raf and Gabs.'

'Who are they?' Malcolm asked.

'Friends,' Zak muttered. And he thought: *my only ones.*

'I can do it,' Malcolm said.

Zak blinked at him. 'Do what?'

'Make them evacuate Buckingham Palace.'

'How?'

'Does it matter?' asked Malcolm.

Zak thought about that. 'You can't leave the flat. You're not strong enough.'

'I don't need to,' said Malcolm. 'All I need is that.' He pointed at the computer.

'Are you going to do something illegal?'

'Yes.'

'Are you going to hurt anybody?'

'No.'

'Fine,' Zak said. 'Do it.'

He left the room. There was a store cupboard in the hallway, in which Zak found a torch. Where he was going, the light of a mobile phone would be no good.

'Harry!' Malcolm called out to him.

Zak put his head round the corner of the room. 'Yes.'

'Good luck.'

Zak nodded. 'You too,' he said. And without another word – without even stopping to arm himself – he left the flat, hurtled down the stairs and burst out onto the rain-soaked street.

Malcolm took a seat at the computer. He winced sharply with the pain of raising his right arm to the keyboard, but once he had rested his fingers on the keys, they were a blur as he typed.

His first action was to direct the browser to his personal ftp site. From there, he downloaded a small program he had written two years ago and used many times since. As the file was downloading, he brought up a list of the top 100 Twitter users worldwide. The first five were pop stars. Number six was the US president. More pop stars after that. The truth was that it didn't matter who they were. Once he had hacked into a few of these accounts – a trivial matter for him – and used the accounts to tweet the same message, that message would go viral. Worldwide, hundreds of millions of people would be reading it within seconds. The message would be impossible to ignore.

He started at the top. His program hacked the account in approximately fifteen seconds. Malcolm typed his message. *There is an explosive device in Buckingham Palace. It will detonate today. #palacebomb*

Without hesitation, he clicked send.

Within five minutes he had hacked the top ten accounts. He instructed his browser to follow the #palacebomb hashtag. Malcolm couldn't resist a smile when he saw that his message was being retweeted tens of thousands of times a second.

He sat back in his chair and continued to watch it go viral.

Zak headed east.

The roads were surprisingly busy for the small hours, with armed police and soldiers in evidence, grim-faced in the driving rain. It hardly looked like London any more. Or rather, it looked like London in some horrible future.

He pounded towards Victoria, clutching his torch. It took him twenty minutes to reach the station, where he turned north and headed up towards the offices of the *Daily Post*. The lights in the reception area were on, and two rather bored-looking security guards were on duty, both reading newspapers. Standing on the street and looking up, Zak saw that the lights on the seventh floor were also on. It crossed his mind that Hendricks might be there, but he decided it was unlikely. Besides, he didn't have time to look. He needed to concentrate on retracing his steps of the previous day. He remembered how Ludgrove had followed Hendricks west along Delfont Street. They had both been out of sight for a few seconds once they turned left at the end of the road, and Zak had been surprised to see Hendricks walking past the pub and not going into it. Hendricks had crossed the road at the zebra crossing while a taxi had beeped at Zak for stepping out onto the road . . .

He continued to retrace his steps, stopping only to wipe the rain from his face.

He stopped.

On the other side of the road, obscured by the darkness, the rain and the passing of cars and buses, was a figure. His head – camouflaged by a wide-brimmed hat – was down and he wore a heavy raincoat. Zak couldn't see his face, but he was sure the man's gait was familiar. Torn with indecision, he watched the figure hurry up the street in the opposite direction. Then he shook his head. Time was precious. He needed to stick to his guns.

Before long he was approaching the entrance to the dead-end mews. It was here that Ludgrove had spotted Zak following him.

And it was here that Hendricks himself had seemed to disappear into thin air.

Nobody could disappear into thin air, though. There had to be another explanation.

He stepped into the road – Chalker Mews – just as a flash of lightning split the sky overhead, followed by a clap of thunder that made his bones shake. He kept walking, peering left and right in the gloom. There were no doorways, and there was only a single car parked on the left-hand side. At the end of the mews was a high wall – five metres at least, impossible to scale without help. But Zak's intuition told him that Hendricks hadn't headed *up* when he'd disappeared.

He'd headed *down*.

There was a solitary circular manhole cover just in front of the wall. The only one in Chalker Mews, so far as Zak could see. He looked over his shoulder – more out of habit than anxiety. Nobody else was here. He bent over and, as the rain ran down his neck, he dug his fingernails under the rim of the manhole cover.

With rain streaming into his eyes, he levered the metal disc up onto its edge, then let it fall to the side of the manhole. It clanged against the cobblestones.

Zak kneeled at the edge of the hole, switched on his torch and shone it inside.

20
BLACKOUT

The first thing Zak saw by the beam of his torch was a ladder. It was not built into the cavity to which this manhole gave access, but propped up against an underground brick wall. An ordinary builder's ladder, not too dirty. Someone had put it there, and recently. It meant Zak was on to something.

Carefully, he lowered himself into the hole, feeling for the steps of the ladder with his feet. Once he'd found them, he climbed down, leaving the manhole open. It didn't give him much light, but it made him feel safer. A bit.

The ladder took him down about three metres. As his feet touched the ground he saw movement from the corner of his eye and heard a scurrying sound as whatever creatures lived down here escaped the glare of his torch. He tried to put the thought of rodents from his mind, but of course that only made them loom large in his imagination. He gritted his teeth and stepped away from the safety of the man-hole cover, where the heavy rain was seeping in.

More movement. More rustling.

He pressed on.

The underground corridor in which he found himself was narrow – less than a metre wide. Zak's skin shrank away from the clammy walls and he had barely walked five metres before he felt the need to pull his T-shirt over his nose because the smell down here was getting worse and worse. The sound of the rain hammering on the road above gradually faded away. The silence was chilling. As he walked further, he started to hear a dripping sound as well as the rustling of rats. It echoed against the underground walls.

After about fifteen metres, he came to a T-junction. He had to make a decision. Left or right?

For a brief moment he was back on St Peter's Crag, at the very beginning of his training. Raf was teaching him how to navigate and Zak had suggested the easy option of using the GPS on his phone. '*GPS is good*,' Raf had said, '*but you can't rely on it.*'

Looked like his Guardian Angels had been right.

Again. He felt a sudden pang. A feeling of dreadful loss. Where were they? What had happened to them? He put those thoughts from his mind. He knew they wouldn't want him to get distracted now. There were more important matters at hand.

He pulled up a mental map of his location. From the route he'd taken from the offices of the *Daily Post*, he figured he was somewhere to the north-west of Victoria Station, and heading east. It meant he needed to turn right.

He took a deep breath. For the second time he was going hunting for an explosive device. He'd been lucky last time. Very lucky. There was no way he could be sure that his luck would hold again. He felt a sudden ache of fear, a moment where his courage almost deserted him. Perhaps he should go back. Leave London. Get to safety. Chances were that his Guardian Angels were dead. Zak ignored these thoughts. He'd made his decision. He turned right.

The corridor widened out. Zak found himself wondering what this network of tunnels was. Sewers? Rainwater sluices? He'd heard people talk about Victorian drains under the streets of London. Maybe that's what these old corridors were. He tried not to think about the weight of bricks above him. He just pressed on.

Time didn't exist down here. He had no idea how long he walked. The tunnel bore round to the right, then opened up into a kind of chamber about half the size of a tennis court. There was no hiding for the rats in here. Even when they scampered away from the torch beam Zak could see their thick, furry bodies and whip-like tails. He set his jaw and continued through this sea of squeaking, scuttling rodents.

Another corridor, bearing round to the left this time and running slightly downhill. Zak was growing used to his surroundings, so he picked up speed.

He stopped.

The corridor had opened out again into another chamber. It was much larger than the previous one – perhaps five times the size, though it was difficult to be sure in the gloom. He could see the outlines of a number of boxes, about two metres high, two metres wide and two metres deep. On top of one of them was an object, about the size of a paperback book, and from which a pale blue glow emanated.

It was a glow much like that which Zak had seen coming from the detonator of the second bomb.

In the Knightsbridge flat, Malcolm Mann stared quietly at the computer screen, monitoring the *#palacebomb* hashtag. In his mind, he saw a globe, and as his simple message was retweeted by millions of people, little dots of light appeared on that imaginary globe, illuminating entire continents.

He considered hacking into the mainframe of GCHQ, the UK Government Communication Headquarters, to see what kind of response his viral campaign was having, but that would take time, and there was, he realized, an easier way. He stood up, wincing on account of the sharp pain that tore through his wounded shoulder. Weakly, he moved over to the television set and switched on BBC News 24. Then he moved over to the window that looked out over the London skyline.

Dark clouds had gathered. As a streak of lightning flashed, it looked as if the sky itself was boiling. Cutting across the skyline, however, he spotted four helicopters. They were heading in the direction of Buckingham Palace.

He heard the news in the background. The reporting was feverish. 'The body found hanging from Westminster Bridge has been identified as one Joshua Ludgrove . . . the Chief Commissioner of the Metropolitan Police has urged Londoners to remain highly vigilant . . .' But there was no breaking news. No word of this new disturbance in the skies above the capital. Malcolm understood what that meant. There had been a news blackout. His plan was working.

And his job, he decided, was done.

He looked around. This was a safe place, he supposed, but how long would it *remain* safe? He was in danger of his life, that much was clear. Harry had promised to help him, but now he'd gone chasing bombs and that was a suicide mission. No, he had only himself to rely on. There was no way, *absolutely* no way, he was going to let them send him back to the secure hospital. He'd rather die. His decision was made. He saw no reason to linger. Rather weakly, he left the apartment. Moments later, he was walking down the empty street into the night, just another faceless member of the public in a city gripped by terror.

Rodney Hendricks stood halfway up the Mall, leaning against a lamppost. He was wet through, but he hardly felt it.

Lightning zigzagged across the sky. It lit up the flagpole on the top of the palace, and Hendricks saw the Union Jack hanging limply in the rain. He allowed himself a grim smile. If this morning's operation went particularly well, perhaps the flags of London would soon be hanging at half-mast as the country mourned the death of its Queen.

From here he had a perfect view of the palace, at a safe enough distance to avoid the fallout. He would watch the fruits of his labour, then return to his flat safe in the knowledge that he would have a great deal more funds at his disposal. This was just the beginning.

He watched, and waited. The show was about to begin.

But then he caught his breath.

Shapes were emerging from the rain-filled sky. Three – no, four – silhouettes, suddenly hovering above the high walls of the palace.

Helicopters.

His excitement turned to nausea as he saw figures fast-roping from the aircraft onto the roof of the palace.

Hendricks restrained the howl that came to his lips. He kept watching as the choppers, having delivered their human cargo, rose higher into the air and started to circle.

He checked the time. Less than ten minutes to go. He calmed himself. With any luck, the arrival of these newcomers would do nothing but add to the collateral damage of the explosion.

Another flash of lightning.

A crack of thunder.

The rain continued to fall.

Time continued to tick.

The watcher continued to watch.

* * *

Under other circumstances that glow of the detonator would have seized all Zak's attention, but suddenly there was a voice echoing around the chamber. '*Hendricks! Hendricks! Is that you?*'

Zak's immediate instinct was to switch off the torch and plunge the chamber into near darkness. But even as he did so, he knew he recognized that voice.

'Raf?' he called.

There was a silence.

And then, two voices, a male and a female: '*Zak?*'

Zak turned the torch on again and held it above his head. Twenty metres from his position he saw two figures sitting on the ground, their backs up against some kind of post, twisting their heads away from the dazzling beam of light.

The moment of astonishment – of relief – passed quickly. There wasn't time for that, and the tone of their voices told him there was little to be relieved about. 'Walk carefully, Zak,' Raf called. 'We're surrounded by explosives.'

'How much longer on the timer?' he asked, tersely.

A brief pause.

'Seven minutes. Don't get too close to us. We're tied to pressure pads. And no heroics, Zak. Just do exactly what I tell you to.'

Zak lowered the beam of the torch to the ground. He stepped carefully forward. One pace. Two. Three. He found himself between two of the enormous crates.

'OK, Zak,' Raf said. 'Listen carefully. Hendricks was down here. He's the bomber.'

'I know. Hendricks isn't his real name. He's called—'

'We haven't got time for that. Listen. He told us that detonator is booby-trapped. If we try to defuse it, it'll go off.'

'Then what are we going to do?' Zak breathed. It was cold down here, but he realized he was sweating.

'While he was talking, I tried to examine his set-up as best I could. I want you to approach the crate that has the detonator. I think I saw single wires leading from that crate to each of the others. Am I right?'

Zak did as he was told. As he edged round the central crate, the details of the clock face came into view.

00:07:01
00:07:00
00:06:59

He tried to focus on the job in hand, and not on

the time that felt like it was slipping through his fingers. Raf was right. He counted nine wires, creeping like spiders' legs down the side of the central crate, one leading to each of the others.

'I've got them,' he said.

'Good. I don't think it's going to be possible to defuse the central crate if that's attached directly to the booby-trapped detonator. But I think there's a high chance that we can minimize the damage the blast is going to cause up above if we sever each of those wires to stop the charge carrying to the other crates. Do you have a knife?'

'No,' Zak breathed. Raf swore under his breath, but then Zak remembered something. He dug his hand into his pocket and pulled out Gabs's star-shaped hairpin. He held it up in the light. 'Yours?' he asked Gabs.

'Mine,' Gabs whispered, an awed relief in her voice.

Zak took one of the wires in his left hand and held the sharp edge with which he had cut himself to it. He was about to slice through the wire when Raf spoke again.

'Zak?'

'Yeah?'

'This is just a guess. You understand that, don't you? I can't promise that cutting that wire won't activate the booby trap.'

Zak looked over at his shoulder at his Guardian Angels. They were both staring anxiously at it.

'I thought you were both dead,' he said.

A pause.

'We will be soon, sweetie,' said Gabs.

Her words were like a trigger. Zak's eyes went flat. He looked back down at the wire.

And then he cut it.

There was silence.

'It's done,' he said.

'Cut the other wires,' Raf instructed, but Zak was already on it. He carefully cut the second, and the third. No explosion. Within a minute, he had severed all nine wires. He looked up at the clock – five minutes and three seconds – before turning back to Raf and Gabs. They looked haunted.

'You need to go now, sweetie,' Gabs said. 'Get out of here as quickly as you can.'

Zak ignored her. He picked up his torch and shone it at their feet. The pressure pads on which they were sitting were simply two sheets of metal. He didn't know what kind of mechanism was underneath the sheets themselves, but a mess of coloured wires sprouted from each one, leading up to the central crate and the detonator.

'I told you, Zak,' Raf said, his voice dangerously low, 'no heroics. You need to catch up with

Hendricks, to stop him doing this again . . .'

But Zak had turned his back on them. He ran to the nearest of the crates of explosives – it was about fifteen metres from Raf and Gabs's position – and rapped his fist against the wood. It was thin, flimsy balsa wood. It needed to be, Zak realized, so that it didn't deaden the blast at all. He clutched the diamond star firmly in his right hand and cut along the grain of one of the side panels. The blade sliced easily into it, scoring a line twenty centimetres long through the wood and into the crates deadly contents.

'*Zak!*' Gabs urged. '*Go!*'

He kept his back to his Guardian Angels and scored another line parallel to the first. With a little more difficulty, he cut against the grain at either end of the parallel lines. The wood fell away to reveal a rectangular hole. Zak wormed his fingers behind the lower edge of the hole, steadied his right foot against the bottom of the crate, and pulled as hard as he could.

The flimsy wood around the crate splintered and broke. The noise echoed around the chamber, clearly scaring the rats by the sudden chorus of squeaking that filled the space. Raf and Gabs were shouting at him, but he barely heard them as, ignoring the splinters in his sore, dirty hands, he continued to rip the crate to shreds. Within forty-five seconds, he had pulled away one entire side, and was shining his torch at it to see what he had revealed.

The plastic explosives inside the crate were neatly stacked. Little parcels of death, each one the size of a brick. They were about as heavy as a brick too. Zak piled six of them in his arms, then headed back to where Raf and Gabs were standing. They were silent now, staring at him in blank astonishment as he carefully laid the cakes of plastic explosive around Gabs's feet.

He ran back to the open crate, glancing at the clock as he went. Three minutes and counting. He grabbed another armful of explosives, ran back and added them to the stockpile.

It was only when he had deposited a third armful that he pulled the diamond star from his pocket and cut the ropes binding Gabs's wrists and ankles.

'Stand up slowly and then step off,' he told her. 'The weight of the explosives should keep the pressure plate down.'

Gabs looked over at Raf. He nodded once.

And then she rose carefully to her feet, wincing as her stiff muscles protested, then stepped over the explosives and onto the solid floor.

Zak saw the pressure plate move – a faint wobble. One of the cakes of explosive tumbled from the top of its pile and his heart almost stopped. But then it fell still. It had worked.

Time check.

00:02:17

'Help me,' he told Gabs. She didn't need telling twice. They ran over to the open crate and filled their arms with more cakes of explosive, before depositing them around Raf's feet. A second trip and they were done. Zak cut the ropes that bound him, then held his breath as his friend slowly stood up, then stepped over the weights.

00:01:23

'Let's get out of here!' Raf barked. *'There's nothing else we can do . . .'*

Zak led the way, his torch lighting their path. He ran like he was in a dream, urging his legs to move quickly, but never feeling he was going as fast as he could. With every pace he took, he expected to hear the explosion behind him. All they could do was hope that only the central crate would detonate, and that the force of the blast would not cause the remainder to blow up. But even then, it was going to be a blast to write home about.

It came without warning, just as Zak was entering the first, smaller chamber. He heard the sound of the explosion first – a low, monstrous rumble that echoed ominously around the chamber – before the shock wave hit him. It was as forceful as if somebody had struck him squarely in the back with a heavy, blunt instrument. Zak flew forward at least two metres, before landing on his front and scraping his face against the hard, wet floor. He ignored the sudden flood of terrified rodents that shrieked past and over him, turning instead to check that Gabs and Raf were OK.

They weren't.

Hendricks looked at his watch. Ten seconds to go. His skin tingled. It wasn't because he was cold or wet. It was more elemental than that. In ten seconds, the moment for which he had been waiting for years would come to fruition, and he was here to watch it happen.

Five seconds.

A single chopper rose up from the gardens of Buckingham Palace. Hendricks watched it with a frown. Was it carrying a precious cargo? He imagined so, and the thought made him bitter. But he did not allow himself to become disheartened. The building was the thing. The crumbling of the palace would be an image as potent as 9/11.

Two seconds to go.

One second.

Zero.

There was a rumble. Hendricks heard it quite clearly. Like a distant earthquake, or maybe that was just what he wanted to believe. He narrowed his eyes, waiting for the building to collapse in on itself. He had planned it carefully, each crate of explosives precisely positioned to cause maximum impact.

Nothing happened.

Give it time, he told himself. *It will take a while, once the foundations are destroyed, to see the effects.*

He *gave* it time.

Still nothing happened.

A hot surge of anger rose in his gut. It was impossible. *Impossible*. The fools in the underground chamber were in no position to compromise the device, and he knew he had made no mistake in its construction. And yet, *nothing had happened*.

A red mist descended. He found himself striding towards the palace. Unbidden, a face had arisen in his mind. A young teenager. Tall for his age. Unruly hair. He had said his name was Harry Gold, but Hendricks was beginning to have his doubts about that. He knew better than anyone how easily a name could be changed.

And he knew how easily a person could be killed. He had seen it happen enough times, after all.

* * *

Gabs had made it into the chamber but had been thrown to the floor just like Zak. She jumped up again, cat-like, and looked back just in time to see the tunnel from which they had emerged collapsing. '*Raf!*' she screamed, as both she and Zak threw themselves in the direction of the rubble collapsing above him. '*RAF!*'

Bricks showered down from the ceiling, a solid version of the rain that had soaked Zak outside. It continued for about five seconds, after which there was a sudden, terrible silence. The entrance to the tunnel was entirely blocked. There was no sign of their friend.

Neither Zak nor Gabs needed to say a word. They grabbed chunks of brick and rock from the mouth of the tunnel. The debris was immensely heavy, and Zak felt the muscles in his arms and across his chest harden as he strained to move the larger pieces.

A minute of heavy labour passed when, ten metres into the chamber, there was another shower of rubble. They continued to work as if they hadn't heard the sound, but when it happened again thirty seconds later, it couldn't go unremarked upon. 'Ceiling's collapsing,' Gabs rasped, her voice like sandpaper. 'If you want to go, go.' She didn't look at

Zak as she said it, nor did she sound at all hopeful that he would take her up on the suggestion. Zak didn't reply. He just carried on working, relentlessly dragging and pulling the fallen rubble away from the mouth of the tunnel.

They saw Raf's hand first. It was poking out from a gap between two boulders, and it was deadly still.

'Raf . . .' Gabs whispered.

There was no reply.

They redoubled their efforts. Zak tore away a boulder which, if adrenalin hadn't been surging through his veins, he wasn't sure he'd have been able to budge. It revealed Raf's forearm, his sleeve ripped and the skin scratched and bloodied. And still not moving. Gabs went into a frenzy, scrabbling at the rubble, pulling it away from the area around Raf's arm, throwing it behind her as if it was made of polystyrene. Her lips were moving but no sound came from them. It was almost as if she was muttering a silent prayer.

And suddenly, her prayer was answered.

Raf's arm moved. The fingers clenched then spread out again. The forearm bent at the elbow. Moments later, Zak pulled away a rock that revealed his torso, and another that revealed his head. He had fallen on his side and his face was streaked with blood. He looked dazed, almost as though he was wondering where he was and how he had got there.

The sound of more rubble falling from the ceiling of the chamber brought him to his senses, however. 'We need to get out of here,' Zak told him. He grabbed Raf's arm and helped his friend as he clambered through the gap they had made. Shining his torch into the chamber, Zak's stomach turned as he saw a curtain of debris showering down just metres from them.

'*RUN!*' Gabs shouted.

And so they did, covering their heads with their hands as they sprinted through the solid rain, to the other side of the chamber and into the tunnel again.

It felt smaller. More claustrophobic. The ceiling lower, the walls narrower. Or maybe that was just Zak. He couldn't run fast enough. When they arrived back at the T-junction, he yelled at the others to take a left-hand turn, and he had seldom felt so relieved as when he saw the open cover of the manhole, and the heavy rain sluicing into it. He scrambled up the ladder into the open air, then leaned over to help Raf and Gabs up.

But as he did so, he heard a click and felt something hard and cold against the back of his head.

'Stand up very slowly,' said a voice. 'I want your hands where I can see them. Any sharp moves, my young friend, and I promise I will not hesitate to kill you.'

Zak swallowed hard. He stood up slowly, his hands in the air, his palms outstretched.

'Turn around,' said the voice.

Zak did as he was told, to find himself face to face with Rodney Hendricks. He had a handgun pointed at Zak's forehead, and he had murder in his eyes.

21

MURDER IN HIS EYES

'Harry Gold.' Hendricks spoke in little more than a whisper.

'Lee Herder,' Zak replied.

Hendricks's eyes narrowed. 'How did you find out?'

Zak didn't answer immediately. He forced himself not to look towards the manhole. He wanted to give Hendricks no clue that Raf and Gabs were down there. If Hendricks thought they were dead – which he no doubt did – he wouldn't hesitate to shoot them if they turned up alive. He just prayed they heard what was happening.

'Ludgrove was investigating your brother's death,' Zak told him. 'He was a good reporter.'

Hendricks sneered. 'He was too close to working out who I really was. That's why he had to go. He won't be meddling in anybody else's affairs.' His little round glasses were covered in raindrops. His beard was wet and dripping.

Keep him talking, Zak thought to himself. *As long as he's talking, he's not shooting.* 'Yeah,' he said. 'I noticed that. I can't help wondering how you lured him to Westminster Bridge.'

'I guess you'll have to carry on wondering,' said Hendricks. 'How did you know where the bombs were?'

'The long-tailed shrike,' Zak breathed. 'Your codes were easy to crack if you knew where to look for them. What I don't understand is why you put them out there in the first place.'

Hendricks gave a mirthless snort of laughter. Zak noticed that his gun hand was shaking slightly.

There was no movement from the manhole. Raf and Gabs clearly knew not to emerge. The hole itself was immediately to his nine o'clock. Hendricks was two metres away to his twelve o'clock. He had lowered his gun slightly so that it was pointing at Zak's chest.

'You don't need to know that, Harry Gold,' Hendricks breathed. 'It hardly matters to you any more, in any case.'

Zak stepped backwards, away from Hendricks. One pace. Two paces. Hendricks's hand was still shaking. *He's a coward,* Zak told himself. *He prefers to massacre people with a bomb than to get his hands dirty . . .*

Hendricks didn't lower the gun, but he stepped forward. He was next to the manhole cover now. When a clap of thunder cracked overhead, his hand jolted along with his frightened body.

There was movement behind Hendricks. A vehicle turned into Chalker Mews. Its headlamps were on full beam. They lit up the heavy rain and cast long shadows along the cobbled street. At first, Zak thought the vehicle had stopped, but after a couple of seconds he realized it was moving slowly towards them. Hendricks surely knew it was there. He had to be able to see how the headlamps cast both his shadow and Zak's against the back wall of the mews. Its arrival, however, didn't seem to surprise or concern him. Zak could only assume he was expecting it. And that couldn't be good news.

Zak stepped backwards again, another two paces. 'Please don't kill me,' he whispered.

Hendricks advanced once more, just as Zak had hoped he would. That was his mistake.

The manhole was behind him now. Out of sight. Zak grabbed his chance. *'Now!'* he shouted.

A look of confusion crossed Hendricks's face. What did the boy mean? It was only at the very last second that he realized the instruction wasn't meant for him. By then it was too late. Gabs had emerged from the manhole in absolute silence, like a snake from a jar. Only the upper half of her body was above ground level, but that was enough. She leaned towards Hendricks and hooked an arm around one of his ankles. Then she tugged.

A shot rang out from Hendricks's weapon, but he was already falling as he fired. The round sped harmlessly past Zak's right thigh and embedded itself in the brick wall behind him. Hendricks hit the ground. He tried to regroup, to aim in Zak's direction once more, but Zak was too quick for him. He lurched forward and kicked the weapon from his assailant's hand. It clattered across the cobblestones as Gabs emerged fully from the manhole, followed immediately by Raf.

Hendricks started crawling away, desperately trying to get his hands back on the weapon, but Raf was on him in an instant. He grabbed him by his thinning hair and pulled him to his feet. Hendricks cried out in pain as Gabs shot past him and retrieved the handgun. Zak's attention, however, was elsewhere.

The vehicle in Chalker Mews was now about twenty metres away from their position. Its lights were still blindingly bright – Zak had to squint to look at it – but the car itself had come to a halt. A door opened on either side and four figures stepped out into the rain.

To Zak, blinded by the glare of the headlamps, they were little more than shadows. He could, however, make out the silhouettes of their weapons. They were not carrying handguns like Hendricks, but sub-machine guns, and they were raising them in the direction of the quartet at the end of the mews.

Zak felt a moment of relief. Armed response. They were safe. But then he saw Hendricks's face. There was a cruel gleam of elation, and in that instant Zak realized that these gunmen were not here to help him, Raf and Gabs. They were the enemy.

'*GET DOWN!*' he roared, flinging himself to the ground as he did so. His Guardian Angels reacted immediately, slamming their bodies down against the cobbles. They hit the dirt just in time. Three individual shots rang out, and Zak felt the displacement of air as a round flew a metre directly above where he was hugging the ground.

Two more shots, but from Gabs this time. Her aim was accurate and each round shattered one of the vehicle's headlamps, plunging Chalker Mews back into sudden darkness.

More gunfire from beside the vehicle, but because the lights were out their aim was now awry. Zak and his Guardian Angels moved with one thought. Forget Hendricks: get to safety. He rolled along the wet cobbles towards the manhole. Once he reached it, he didn't bother with the ladder, but just jumped back down into the relative safety of the tunnel before hurling himself out of the way to give Raf and Gabs the chance to follow suit. Raf came first, landing heavily on the ground. Gabs followed immediately afterwards. She was altogether more fleet of foot – as she hit the ground, she was already twisting her body around and aiming the handgun back up through the manhole. She fired a warning shot out onto the street, then fell to one knee, her gun arm stretched out, ready to fire on anyone who appeared in her field of view.

Silence. Just the rain.

And then the squealing of tyres up above, growing louder. In his mind, Zak saw the vehicle speeding up to the manhole before it screeched to a halt. A clatter of footsteps, and then a voice with a heavy European accent reached their hiding place. 'All right, Hendricks, in the car. *Vamos.*' The man spoke Spanish.

'Where . . . where are we going?' Hendricks's voice was flustered.

'He wants to speak to you.'

'Who?'

'Who do you think, idiot? Señor Martinez, of course.'

A scuffling sound. Shadows fell across the open manhole. Gabs kept her arm straight and her aim true, but nobody entered her line of fire.

Zak heard the noise of doors slamming shut, and the vehicle reversing at great speed. And then there was silence once more.

Simply the rain on the cobbles, and the frenzied beating of his heart.

The interior of the car that ushered Rodney Hendricks away from Chalker Mews was very warm. So warm that his wet clothes started to steam, and his skin to itch. But he wasn't paying attention to the steam or the soreness. He was paying attention to the armed men, one on either side, two in the front. They didn't speak to him. They didn't even look at him.

'Where are we going?' he asked.

No answer.

'I *demand* that you tell me where we are going.'

The gunman to his right finally honoured him with a stare. His lip curled. *You are in no position to demand anything*, he seemed to say, though in reality he said nothing.

The vehicle with no headlamps attracted warning horns from other cars. After about three minutes, the driver pulled into a side street and stopped. All four armed men climbed out. One of them pulled Hendricks's arm to indicate that he should do the same.

A Land Cruiser was parked just ahead of them. A gunman opened the rear door and pushed Hendricks into the back seat, where somebody was waiting for him.

He was a thin young man. Not much older, Hendricks thought, than Harry Gold himself. There was a cold, cruel light in his eyes, and he remained silent until the gunmen had climbed into the vehicle and it had eased back into the traffic. Even then, his words were few and carefully chosen.

'I confess myself disappointed,' said the young man. 'Your campaign has not been a success.' His perfect English bore only the trace of a Spanish accent.

'I wouldn't say that, Señor Martinez,' Hendricks mumbled.

'What *would* you say?'

'The first bomb did what it was intended to do. The second bomb too, even though the hospital was evacuated.'

Silence.

Hendricks found himself stuttering. 'The third . . . the third device was compromised.'

'Indeed?'

By chance – or perhaps by design – they had just arrived at Buckingham Palace. There was heavy security at the gates, but it was perfectly intact. Señor Martinez looked at it meaningfully.

Hendricks was sweating into his damp clothes. He looked straight ahead, through the windscreen, as the Land Cruiser continued to drive.

'I gave you a considerable sum of money, Mr Hendricks. Our agreement was quite clear. You target three locations in London. One to target the transport system, as has been done before to great effect. One to show you are able to kill even the most innocent in your society if necessary to achieve your aims. And one of your own choice. To prove your ingenuity to me, you announce in advance the location of each explosion by one of the methods we discussed. Should you manage to make the covert announcement *and* successfully detonate the bombs, I would know that you were sufficiently skilful to be part of my organization. I would then continue to fund your little hobby. You have your reasons for wanting to target the people of the UK – reasons in which I have no particular interest – and

I have mine. It could have been a match made in heaven. Unfortunately, we failed to discuss what would happen if you did *not* manage to carry this operation out to my satisfaction. I think that is a discussion we ought to have now, don't you?'

Hendricks gave a barely noticeable nod.

'How is it,' the young man breathed, 'that you came to fail so pathetically?'

'The code,' Hendricks whispered. 'Someone cracked it. A . . . a boy. But I know his name. I can bring him to you. He is called Gold . . . Harry Gold . . .'

Hendricks felt the young man's body stiffen.

'Are you trying to mock me?' he breathed.

Hendricks hardly knew what to say. 'Of . . . of course not, Señor Martinez.'

'Stop the car somewhere private,' the young man told his driver.

'Wh . . . what for?' asked Hendricks.

'So that we can continue our delightful conversation.' He didn't sound as though he found the conversation at all delightful. His voice was flat and monotone. There was a dead look in his eyes as the car crossed a bridge then took a small, badly kept road that meandered down to the edge of the river. It came to a halt and one of the gunmen opened the rear door again. He gave Hendricks an unfriendly nod to indicate that he should climb out. 'Leave us,' Señor Martinez told his guards once they were both outside the vehicle.

They were alone now, standing in the rain on the bank of the Thames, the ground underfoot oozing mud. London glowed on the other side of the river – the Houses of Parliament, the Eye – but here it was dark, gloomy and deserted.

The young man drew a gun. Hendricks stepped back, but slipped on the treacherous ground and fell clumsily. The tall teenager towered over him, his gun arm stretched out, the weapon pointing in his direction.

'There is no room for failure in my organization, Mr Hendricks,' he shouted over the noise of the rain. 'And there is no room for anybody who might be in a position to tell Harry Gold that I am still alive.' He stared at Hendricks, his eyes narrow and hard. 'Harry and I, we have . . . history,' he added. 'Mexico, Africa . . . and the death of my father. Harry believes that *I* am dead. But as you can see, I am very much alive.'

Hendricks looked at him, confusion for a moment pushing fear from his face. 'I . . . I don't understand,' he shouted. And then, when he saw the total lack of expression on the young man's face, 'I would never tell Harry Gold anything about you.

I'll even kill him for you, if you like.'

The young man shook his head. 'No,' he said. 'I will be the one to kill Harry Gold. This I have sworn.' For the first time, a faint smile crossed his lips. 'So I suppose I need a little bit of practice.'

Hendricks shook his head. He tried to crawl away, but could not get a grip in the mud. 'Please,' he begged in a hoarse voice. '*Please* . . .'

The young man inclined his head and looked almost curiously at his prey. Then he fired three shots.

The first hit Hendricks in the stomach. The second in the neck. It was the third that killed him, blasting away a sizeable chunk of his skull and spattering the grey brain matter over the already oozing ground.

Hendricks's body twitched, then fell limp. The rain continued to fall, and the dirty water of the rising tide lapped gently against his corpse.

The young man returned to his car, his face lost in thought. He did not speak to his guards, and they knew better than to speak to him, or to mention the blood spatter on his wet clothes. They were a silent party as they drove south, out of London and into the countryside beyond.

EPILOGUE

One week later

On a windswept island off the coast of Scotland, a boy looked out to sea.

Zak Darke had not trained since returning to St Peter's Crag, nor had he taken any lessons. Raf and Gabs had not said to him that their work was suspended, but they clearly did not have the stomach for it either. When Zak had told them about Michael's injury, they had grown pale. And now, on the rare occasions that they spoke, they avoided the subject. They hid their anxiety with awkward conversations about the weather. There was no concrete news from anyone higher up in the organization, no confirmation that their handler was either dead or alive. 'You mustn't blame yourself, sweetie,' Gabs had whispered when he'd told them what had happened at the warehouse. But that was

315

easy to say and less easy to do. Guilt was all Zak felt. Nothing would make it go.

Gazing from the window in his bedroom, he narrowed his eyes. Through the mist surrounding the island, he saw something in the sky. A shadow, which disappeared as quickly as it had appeared. It could have been anything: a bird, a cloud formation. Zak sprinted from his room anyway, along the corridor and down the wide staircase that led to the entrance hall. At the front door, he quickly tapped a numeric code, then shot outside and peered into the distance. There was only one way to leave or arrive at this island: by helicopter. Sure enough, a chopper was landing fifty metres from the house. It stayed on the ground for less than a minute. By the time it had lifted off again, a figure had emerged, and now it was limping slowly towards the house with the aid of a stick.

Michael's features did not become clear until he was twenty metres away from the house. By this time, Raf and Gabs had arrived. Gabs ran towards the old man, and even Raf – normally so stern – had a grin on his face. The sight of Michael's thin, pallid face as, helped by Gabs, he limped into the house, was not enough to dampen Zak's sudden elation. Michael was *alive*.

The old man was wheezing by the time he was

sitting in an armchair in his office. Zak, Raf and Gabs waited silently and respectfully for him to regain his breath. They had a thousand questions, but they knew Michael would only answer them in his own time.

He addressed Zak first. 'I have my life to thank you for, Zak. I'll never forget that.' With those words, Zak's guilt lifted. 'Next time you decide to shoot me, however, I'd appreciate it if you used a slightly softer round.'

Zak grinned at him; Michael just winced. From his pocket he pulled a piece of paper. It was a child's crayon drawing, very colourful. At the top of the page was what looked like a black helicopter. A rope was hanging from it, and at the end of the rope a stick man. Underneath, in unsure lettering, were the words 'thank you'.

'From Ruby MacGregor,' Michael said. 'The little girl you and Gabs rescued from the hospital. I'm told she's doing very well.'

Zak stared at the picture. Was that really how other people saw him? He wasn't sure how that made him feel.

Michael's face grew serious again. 'Tell me everything,' he said. And so Zak did. He left nothing out, and when he had finished there was a silence in the room for a full minute. 'It sounds like young Ruby and I are not the only ones who owe you a great deal, Zak. You'll be pleased to know that the explosion under the palace caused no significant damage – all easily repairable and those tunnels are being sealed as we speak – and all relevant principals were evacuated as soon as the news of the bomb had been received, followed rapidly by all others on site, so there were no casualties. Also, no doubt, you'll be intrigued to learn that Rodney Hendricks was found murdered by the banks of the Thames. It seems he was killed the same night he tried to destroy the palace.'

'Why?' Zak asked.

Michael pressed his fingers together. 'Hard to say, Zak. I don't suppose we'll ever know for sure. At a guess, I'd say that his coded messages were aimed at a third party. Perhaps he was trying to prove himself – that not only could he target major landmarks, but that he was also clever enough to reveal where they were, under our noses, without us realizing. He was wrong, of course – thanks to you, and young Malcolm Mann.'

Malcolm. Other than noticing his absence when returning to the flat – and they had spent only hours there before Gabs and Raf had called in to report and the agency had whisked them back up to Scotland – the strange boy had almost slipped Zak's mind. With obvious difficulty, Michael put one hand into her coat and pulled out a photograph. He handed it to Zak. It showed Malcolm. His arm was in a sling, but he was wearing sunglasses and a baseball cap, and walking along a golden beach. 'South Africa,' Michael said, answering the question on Zak's lips. 'And no, I don't know how he got there – although I do believe the four of us – plus the agent who took this photograph – are now the only other people in the world who know that's where he's escaped to. I'll be keeping my eye on him. It may be that we need his particular skill set before long.'

'How's he going to live? I mean, does he have any money?'

'I don't believe he'll have too much difficulty making funds appear in his bank account, do you?'

Zak shook his head, and couldn't help a small smile. It didn't last long. There was another question on his lips. It had been bothering him ever since that night, but he hadn't found the courage to bring it up in front of Raf or Gabs. 'There's something I wanted to ask you,' he said.

Michael inclined his head. Zak had the impression he knew what was coming.

'When they took Hendricks away, they were taking him to see . . .' He looked at the floor. 'To see someone called Martinez,' he said quietly.

There was a pause.

'Martinez is a very common name, Zak,' Michael said.

'I know, but—'

'Cruz Martinez is dead, Zak. You saw him fall into the Atlantic Ocean in the middle of a storm.'

'But what if—'

'Our intelligence networks are very thorough. If Martinez was alive we'd know about it.'

'He's clever,' Zak muttered.

'So are we. He's dead, Zak. Put him from your mind. You have other adversaries now.'

'Michael's right, sweetie,' said Gabs. Her eyes were wide with sympathy, and Raf's solid, dependable face clearly showed that he agreed.

Zak bowed his head. 'Yeah,' he said, 'you're probably right.' He looked around the room. 'I might . . .' He jabbed one thumb in the direction of the door. 'It's good to see you, Michael.'

His Guardian Angels said nothing. They just watched him leave. Zak felt their eyes boring into his back as he left the room and closed the door quietly behind him.

Up in his room, Zak took his place by the window again. They were right, of course. He *had* seen Cruz Martinez plunge into the stormy waves of the

Atlantic. No one could survive that. Why, then, did he feel so unsure? Why was his pulse racing and his skin prickling? Why was it that, as he looked out to sea, he had the unnerving sensation that, somewhere out there – who could say where? – a gangly young man with dark hair was thinking about Zak as intently as Zak was thinking about him?

How long he sat there, these thoughts spinning in his mind, Zak couldn't have said. All he knew was that the sun was setting by the time he closed the curtains and lay down on his bed to rest. Tomorrow was another day. Zak didn't know what it would bring. He only knew he had to be ready.

DECODING MESSAGES

There are several instances of coded messages within the text where you might wish to check you have decoded them correctly.

Turn over to see the decoding process.

NOTE: don't cheat and check out these pages first as you could spoil the story for yourself if you do so!

NUMBERS FOR LETTERS

**The numbers are matched to letters
as follows in this grid:**

A	B	C	D	E	F	G	H	I	J
0	1	2	3	4	5	6	7	8	9

K	L	M	N	O	P	Q	R	S	T
10	11	12	13	14	15	16	17	18	19

U	V	W	X	Y	Z
20	21	22	23	24	25

CHAPTER 2:
ADVANCE/RETREAT

The original message sent, using the first random key, is ADVANCE, and the message is received as: JHCFLLH

To decode this using the new key given, SDJOHLO, the calculations are as follows:

Message received	J	H	C	F	L	L	H
As numbers	9	7	2	5	11	11	7
New random key	S	D	J	O	H	L	O
As numbers	18	3	9	14	7	11	14
Subtract numbers to decode	17	4	19	17	4	0	19
Decoded message	R	E	T	R	E	A	T

CHAPTER 5:
HIDDEN IN PLAIN SIGHT

Using the clues in the crossword grid to decode the message about the second bomb:

Message as one down answer	B	O	M	B	I	N	G
As numbers	1	14	12	1	8	13	6
Random key	O	U	A	K	A	P	I
As numbers	14	20	0	10	0	15	8
Add numbers to code a message	15	8	12	11	8	2	14
Now use the grid above to read the message							

CHAPTER 18:
THE LONG-TAILED SHRIKE

Decoding the message in the Nature Notes column.

	L	O	N	G	T	A	I	L	E	D	S	H	R	I	K	E
Message	L	O	N	G	T	A	I	L	E	D	S	H	R	I	K	E
As numbers	11	14	13	6	19	0	8	11	4	3	18	7	17	8	10	4
Random key (initial letters)	Q	G	P	E	P	N	Y	W	W	J	X	T	U	S	S	A
As numbers	16	6	15	4	15	13	24	22	22	9	23	19	20	18	18	0
Add numbers to code the message	1	20	2	10	8	13	6	7	0	12	15	0	11	0	2	4
Use the grid above to read the message																